BARABBAS

Armando Rodríguez

Unless otherwise noted, all biblical references have been taken from various versions of the Bible, amongst them the NKJV. Note: the text in bold in certain parts of the text reflect the author's emphasis.

BARABBAS

Publish by A.R.M
602 Broad Av
Wilmington Ca. 90744
310-834-9376

www.ensupoder.com
enpoder@yahoo.com

ISBN: **9798640829600**
First Copy 2020
Printed in USA
© 2020 by In His Power
Category: Fiction Novel

Design: Justice art
justiceart@live.com
1-424-203-9018
Copyright ©2017 Justice Art, Co.

Interior Design: Kingdom Editorial
info.editorialreino@gmail.com
+ 1 (956) 509 5558
Copyright ©2020 Kingdom Editorial.

All Rights reserved by Author.
Partial or total reproduction of this book is prohibited by any means (electronic, written or spoken) without previous consent from the author with the exception of footnotes.

INDEX

BARABBAS THE HOPE OF A NATION	5
THE BEGINNING	13
GAMALIEL THE BETRAYER	17
BARABBAS THE THIEF AND THE MURDERER	19
THE MESSAGE OF FREEDOM	23
THE ASSAULT	25
THE PREPARATION	29
THE PLAN	33
BARABBAS ARRESTED	39
THE ELITE	45
BARABBAS AND JOHN MEET	49
DIMAS AND GESTAS THE TWO THIEVES	53
JOHN THE PREACHER AND HIS DEATH	61
JESUS ARRESTED	67
JESUS AND BARABBAS MEET	79
JESUS BARABBAS CONVERSION	87
BARABBAS THE DELIVERER	93

BARABBAS THE HOPE OF A NATION

Rome was the most powerful empire in the world during the time when Barabbas was born. Rome had overthrown and conquered many nations, Israel being among them. Israel had been subject to the Roman government for many years. Barabbas was perceived as a rebel in the eyes of the Roman Empire, however, in the eyes of his people, Israel, he was considered a glimpse of hope. Israel suffered indescribable injustice by the Romans; but they never gave up hope in the promise they had received many years before they were conquered. It was a promise given to their forefathers and confirmed for centuries through prophets. Which promise? The promise that a deliverer would come and save the nation of Israel! The Deliverer would set them free from the oppression of the Roman Empire once and for all. They were God's people, a unique, hand selected heritage.

The difference between Israel and the other nations that had been conquered by the Romans was not the size of the nation; it was the hope in the promise of Israel. When a man loses hope he becomes short sighted and his present condition is his destiny. Hope is the fuel of faith and faith provides the confidence that allows the unseen to become a reality.

Barabbas was born to Aryeh, a Rabbi, a teacher of the law, as a teacher of the law Aryeh shared the hope with his people. He believed that his nation would be liberated. His hope was so real that he named his son Jesus Barabbas which means, **the son of the father, the deliverer**.

Barabbas did not behave like a deliverer; he hated school and refused to study. Known for his temper, he was constantly fighting at school and in his neighborhood. His father spent endless hours attempting to teach Barabbas the Jewish laws, customs, and ancestry. Barabbas wouldn't study and was quite vocal and opinionated about not wanting to study. He brought upon much shame to his family name.

Aryeh decided it was in Barabbas and the family's best interest to send him to military school. He thought, "Surely my son will learn discipline and grow strong in character." The school specialized in armed forces and, knowing his son was always fighting, he was sure the decision to enroll him would lead to success. Barabbas would learn how to fight and defend with purpose.

It pleased Aryeh that the school training was something that gained Barabbas' attention. Specifically, he liked to swing the sword; Barabbas had mastered sword skills and became one of the top of his class. Unfortunately, no training was able to help him with his temper. Continuing to allow his short temper to get the best of him, he found himself constantly fighting with his classmates.

Aryeh was getting older, he felt he would not live much longer, and his only son was still seemingly without direction. Aryeh called for Barabbas and said, "*Barabbas, my days will soon come to an end. I've done my best to deposit inside you the promises of God. I have shared stories with you of our ancestors your entire life. I know you have heard me; you are a smart young man. Never forget that the Lord our God will deliver our nation. This degrading condition that Rome has subjected us to will come to an end. Be patient and hopeful, in patience lies power and in*

TRUTH?... POSSIBLE?... PERHAPS?

hope lies faith for our future". These were the last words spoken by Aryeh before he died. Words of hope and courage.

Barabbas mourned his father and stayed with his mother for a short period of time. Barabbas thought about what his father told him. He struggled with the advice that his father had given him for, within Barabbas patience and hope were nonexistent. Truth be told, Barabbas resented the stories his father shared with him. The stories of how God delivered his people from Pharaoh and how he provided in the desert only caused Barabbas to grow angry and resentful. He questioned God. "*How could a great God allow for His own people to be enslaved? How could He permit Rome to oppress and ridicule the people He called His own? Why so many years of waiting? Did God not care about the injustice and humiliation they were subjected to, day in and day out?*" Though Barabbas never expressed these questions to his father, he knew his father was able to see the doubt in his face. Neither of them addressed what they both felt.

Several years went by after Aryeh's death and the desperation of the people of Israel created more rage for Barabbas. He knew that for a man to find dignity within him he had to be free. How can a man be a man when he is told where to go, what to eat, when to sleep? *How can a man enjoy life when he is restricted? Others are dictating what you are able to have and who you are; how can a man have pride of his ancestry when they are not a nation?* These thoughts tormented Barabbas; the restrictions that were imposed on him and his people caused him to become bitter. He was consumed with the opportunity to be free.

One evening Barabbas was going through his father's belongings and came across a scroll that he hadn't seen before, one of many his father would read to him often; however the scroll Barabbas came across was unfamiliar to him. He curiously began to read it. He was fascinated by what he was learning; he read it once and then again. It was the history of an Israelite King by the name David.

Barabbas was inspired reading of King David's battles and victories. Barabbas read David's victory over the mighty Goliath, he read all of the victories he accomplished with his mighty men. As much as he was moved by what he was learning, he couldn't help but wonder why his father never mentioned King David. He felt as if his father had hid this great jewel from him; but why? Why wouldn't he share with him such amazing exploits? Did his father worry Barabbas would shed blood like King David?

Barabbas felt robbed of his ancestry. His entire life he was taught to be patient, to endure, to hope; listening to the same stories his whole life! And all the while never learning that within his blood line there was a mighty warrior that made a show, openly with the enemies of Israel —a great King that won many battles for his nation. The more he read the scroll the more he questioned why his father never told him about King David.

After many days Barabbas decided to confront his mother with the question (to be determined of more substance). Frustrated and defensive, he asked, "*Mother, why is it that my father never told me about King David? My entire life he only told me about the deliverer, Moses, whom God used to deliver our people from the great nation of Egypt. But I have never learned of King David.*"

His mother was able to see and hear his frustration; desperately she tried to avoid answering the question. She tried to distract his attention by asking, "*Son, you haven't had lunch, are you hungry? Can I make you some-*

TRUTH?... POSSIBLE?... PERHAPS?

thing to eat?" Barabbas frustration quickly turned to annoyance when she didn't provide an answer. He shouted, *"Mother!!! I asked you a specific question and you offer me lunch???!! Please."*

His mother became very still and quietly asked him, *"Where did you hear about King David?"*

Barabbas answered, "I was missing dad and began to go through his scrolls. I foun*d a scroll that was unfamiliar to me. Mother, I read it over and over fascinated by King David's exploits. I beg you, why would father not share such amazing history?"*

His mother could see the desperation in her son. She gently told him, *"Come my son, sit close to me"*. Barabbas reluctantly drew closer to her.

They sat in the living room and she began to explain, *"Son, your father never mentioned King David to you for fear that you would become attracted to King David's methods. Judging by your enthusiasm, your father was right. King David and his mighty men brought peace to our nation; however, the cost was at a high price, many died. Your father kept King David's history hidden from you because knew you would become zealous by King David and would prefer his methods over Moses our deliverer. Moses never swung a sword, yet our people were liberated; King David killed many and shed much blood to bring peace to our nation. I can see in your eyes, my son that you will follow King David's methods, and that is what your father feared."*

Barabbas responded, *"Mother, our people are not a nation! The memory of our nation does not exist! When is anyone going to get it? We are slaves! Blood must be shed!! Unless blood is shed there will be no peace, blood is the price of liberty from bondage!"* Barabbas, irate with the freshness of this betrayal left his mother's house.

TRUTH?... POSSIBLE?... PERHAPS?

That night Barabbas wrote a farewell note to his mother. She would never understand his newly found outlook and the role he needed to take on. Barabbas reasoned within himself that the note was the best way to communicate, so early next morning he slid it under her bedroom door. It would be a long time before he returned to see his mother again.

With a new outlook and mission, Barabbas called upon his school friends that were now grown men, grown men who had been trained and skilled for battle. Barabbas began to speak to them of the marvelous exploits of King David. He inspired them as he had been inspired by the history of King David.

A natural leader, it didn't Barabbas to develop a following. His following growing in numbers and quickly adopting his ideologies, Barabbas and his followers had one mission: freedom from Rome.

Barabbas created secret schools of the sword. His followers taught new recruits how to master the sword and also taught them their message and their newfound cause, "*freedom from Rome*". Young men by the hundreds began to join and follow Barabbas. Barabbas had become the face to freedom and the living hope for his people.

Was Barabbas another false hope for the people? Was Barabbas the real thing? These were the questions that still some of the people once called Israel asked themselves. These thoughts were an emotional rollercoaster for some of them. Everyone wanted to believe but not everyone wanted to set their hopes up. Through the years there had been others before Barabbas, who had rounded up the people only to leave the people broken and disappointed.

Hope is the oxygen to faith and when you cut the hope

of the people you cut their oxygen and damage their faith and if one does not have faith, they lack the freedom to dream.

THE BEGINNING

When the nation of Israel was invaded by Rome, those that were wealthy and respected along with those with social influence, were degraded and humiliated. Their possessions became property of the Roman government and there was little to nothing they could do about it. Their glory became shame and anything or anyone connected to such a lifestyle, that was an Israelite, was introduced to a life of want. The life they had before was like a dream that never happened. The humiliation they were subjected to daily became the natural way of life. They had no choice, they conformed.

The Israelites were treated like second class citizens; they were segregated in the marketplace and every other public setting. This kind of treatment produced in them insecurity, hopelessness, rejection and abandonment.

The type of treatment Rome executed on Israel was imbedded in Barabbas but the way he responded to this oppression was not as most people did. Every time Barabbas witnessed the humiliation of his people was another reason to fight against Rome. Most people lose hope, most people begin to adapt, and once a person accepts their present as their future it becomes their normal routine. Barabbas was not most people. He would not conform.

Barabbas was always different than most people, even at his birth.

The day Barabbas was born his father was working

TRUTH?... POSSIBLE?... PERHAPS?

late. He needed to get some things finished up and he did not get home at his regular time. It was the same day that Barabbas father gave his maid the day off. It was a day that if something could go wrong, it would go wrong!

Barabbas' mother thought that day was going to be just like any another day, her nine months were not yet due, she was entering her seventh month of pregnancy. Barabbas' mother recalls it as if it was yesterday.

It was beautiful spring morning; birds were singing outside as she washed and hung her laundry; she had her whole day ahead of her and lots to do. She cooked morning breakfast for herself and her husband as she had done for the 15 years of their marriage. It was just the two of them. They longed for a child but were unable to have one.

It was shameful for her; a woman was supposed to bear children. Her inability to bear children was a disgrace, a curse even. It didn't help matters that Barabbas's father was a teacher of the law. The constant negative attention and criticism was more than any person could fathom. "*How can a rabbi, a religious minister, not have children? Is it that they're having problems? Is it that they are curse by God?*" Even before Barabbas was born there was conflict and controversy connected to him.

His mother, only just entering her seventh month of pregnancy did not expect a 4-pound Barabbas to be born the day of his birth. his early birth meant no one was there to assist, so she gave birth alone which was an unusual circumstance. Barabbas arrived with his umbilical cord entangled around his neck, nearly dying from strangulation.

When the neighbors heard a baby crying from Ayer's home they quickly ran inside the house and saw that the baby was born. He was so small; his mother was comforting him. They congratulated her and asked what she would name him she told them her husband would name the child. As she was speaking Aryeh walked in the door. He was in such a haste he walked straight to the kitchen to warm up some food for his wife, he never noticed the people inside. There was a faint squeal that got louder in the house, he looked up from his steaming pot and listened closely for the sound. It was a baby crying, the baby he had longed for. As he heard the child's cry his heart filled with emotion and his eyes swelled with tears as he made his way towards the cry of the baby. He was overwhelmed with joy, he was so engaged at the sight of his child he couldn't hear the neighbors asking him, "What will his name be?"

Finally, he calmed down from the emotional high and answered, "*He will be called Barabbas, Jesus Barabbas. This name means the son of the father, the deliverer.*"

Barabbas father always held on to the promise of their God, that their God would send a deliverer to free Israel.

TRUTH?... POSSIBLE?... PERHAPS?

GAMALIEL THE BETRAYER

Gamaliel was a religious leader who had a reputation as a betrayer among the people of Israel. There was a time Gamaliel was held with the upmost respect among the nation of Israel. He was a doctor of the law and very influential among the Jews and religious leaders, Rome used him as an informant after the overthrowing of Israel. He was no longer a threat to Rome but an asset to the most powerful empire.

The Roman army was becoming concerned with the rumors of Barabbas and his band of followers spreading. It was Gamaliel who had informed Rome of the news of an upcoming leader, Barabbas. During a meeting Gamaliel advised the Roman leaders not to worry. His words were calm and collective, "*Council and dignitaries may the words concerning this Barabbas not trouble you. Not long ago there arose up a Theudas, boasting himself to be somebody; to whom a number of men, about four hundred, joined themselves. Theudas was killed and all who obeyed him, were scattered, and brought to nothing. After this man rose up Judas of Galilee in the days of the taxing and drew away many people after him; he also perished and all who obeyed him were dispersed and I believe that Barabbas will suffer the same fate.*"

How accurate was Gamaliel about Barabbas... or was he? Was it that Gamaliel himself deep down in his heart still believed the prophecies of his ancestors that spoke of one coming and bringing salvation to the nation of Israel? Was

TRUTH?... POSSIBLE?... PERHAPS?

it possible that the position of prestige that Rome granted Gamaliel was not enough to sway his loyalty from Israel? Gamaliel was a doctor of the law, eloquent in speech and full of knowledge. When he was given the choice by Rome to join them or die, death was not an option. He had a great love for his nation, but courage was absent in his heart. As far as Gamaliel was concerned prestige looks better then shame.

Gamaliel had gone to the best schools of his time. The schools however were out of touch with the local people; anyone who wanted to be effective and influential must never be out of touch with the local people. To know them, it was necessary to walk among them. Gamaliel, uptight and haughty, was unwilling to walk amongst his people.

Gamaliel had chosen the high places of the intellectual world of prestige to be his dwelling place. For this very reason Rome did not consider Gamaliel to be a threat because he was easily bribed and manipulated, Rome considered him a betrayer of his own people and so did the Israelites.

Barabbas grew in favor among the people of Israel. When a nation is in its darkest moments, hope is what the people seek and they had found it in Barabbas; one like them, full of scorn towards Rome. Barabbas was more radical than the others that had come before him; he was a radical revolutionary that believed in the power of the sword and therefore different from the others before him.

Gamaliel, although considered a betrayer by his own people, held some loyalty to his people. After all Gamaliel had relatives that reminded him of his roots and regardless of how much prestige and position Rome had given him at the end of the day when Gamaliel would look himself in the mirror, he was still an Israelite.

TRUTH?... POSSIBLE?... PERHAPS?

BARABBAS THE THIEF AND THE MURDERER

To some Barabbas was a glimpse of hope, a hero. To others, he was a thief and a murderer. What a contrast of opinions, what a reputation for someone whose name meant, **the son of the father, the deliverer**. His father or mother never thought their boy would turn out this way. He was just a young innocent boy, the boy they had longed for all of their life. But as life would have it, what at one time was considered innocent, this young man had become one of the most wanted men by Rome.

Barabbas had become a thief and a murderer for the cause that he was fighting—FREEDOM. His revolutionary cause could not survive without funding, especially as his following increased. He quickly found out that every cause had a price other than leading people. He had to provide for the people the swords and the equipment necessary. Which warrior goes to war on own his expense?

Barabbas was thirsty for freedom and his thirst overrode the need to follow the rules. His desperation and his ambition were what fed the vision of his movement which, eventually, led him to become a murderer.

In Rome there was a law for all Israelites, which was that whenever they were commanded by a Roman soldier to do anything it must be obeyed. There was a particular law that dictated that if a Roman soldier asked an Israelite to carry their luggage the Israelite must obey. If they disobeyed, they risked being beaten and put in prison.

TRUTH?... POSSIBLE?... PERHAPS?

Barabbas was not the best person to be around when this law was exercised; a Roman soldier found out the hard way. Barabbas and Zachariah, a much older colleague in age, were traveling to a nearby town. Zachariah was ordered by a Roman soldier to carry his bag; the bag was extremely heavy, but by law there was no way around it, so Zachariah complied. Barabbas was ignited with rage. He hated the injustice to humanity.

The timing for Barabbas to make a point was not good, the plan to overtake Rome was not far. Zachariah locked eyes on Barabbas as with a look that was pleading, "*Don't do anything dumb!" However, the only expression Barabbas saw in his companion's eyes was, "I can't go on! Help me!*"

They continued along the road with the soldier and his belongings, the bag Zachariah was carrying ripped and the soldier's possessions spilled onto the ground. That infuriated the Roman soldier screamed profanities and began swinging the rod he had in his hand striking Zacharias over and over on the head. He shouted, "**Look what you have done! You filthy pig! You're a good for nothing old man!**"

Poor Zacharias, he did not know what was happening he found himself on the floor; all he could do was cover his head and face as the Roman soldier continued to beat upon him with the rod.

Everything happened so fast that Barabbas didn't have time to think but only to react; his instant reaction was not defensive but retaliation against the Roman soldier. Immediately, without a second thought Barabbas went behind the soldier and with one strike of his concealed sword slit the soldier's neck, killing him. He stood over him in shock, the blood of the Roman soldier dripping from his sword, which he held with a tight grip. He could hear Zachariah calling his name. He sounded so far away. "*Barabbas! Barabbas!*" he cried at the top of his voice, but Barabbas just stood there, in shock, he heard the voice of Zachariah as if it were a mile away. Barabbas was the leader of the revolutionary group; however, he had never killed anyone.

For some strange reason as he was standing still in a daze of what just had occurred, he began to experience a new feeling. Was it the feeling of freedom that he always desired for himself and for his people? Or was it the feeling of revenge that made him feel fulfilled and complete? Why did the soldier's blood dripping from his sword and his fist feel liberating? Whatever that feeling was, he liked it. Zacharias still screaming, "*Barabbas, Barabbas let's go, let's get out of here!*"

Barabbas calmly turned around and with a calm voice said, "*Let's go our way*". Barabbas did not run from that scene; he calmly walked away with a distressed Zacharias. Barabbas was not finished savoring the moment and enjoying the feeling he had just experienced.

Killing the Roman soldier was only the beginning of the reputation that Barabbas would build. He never would have imagined what rumors would create; it was as if he added fuel not only to his thirst and hunger for freedom but, surprisingly, seemed to provide hope among the locals and quickly his fame spread and increased.

Many young men joined the revolutionary movement that Barabbas was leading. This time the recruiting was different, he didn't have to go looking for them to recruit them; they came to him and brought others with them! Even the older folks would help by feeding or hiding the young men of the revolutionary movement. The increased support was a fresh breeze of hope to Barabbas, but with great power comes responsibility; they needed weapons, lots of weapons. Barabbas carried the weight of the need for supplies in order to succeed. People can gather together quite easily but once they are together, they need direction and inspiration to move forward. He realized he didn't need any more men, he needed money. He developed a plan to bring in the money for weapons and equipment.

THE MESSAGE OF FREEDOM

Although Barabbas was not an eloquent speaker, his message made up for it, for you see, freedom belongs to one race only; the human race and this, Barabbas understood. "*Freedom!*" cried out Barabbas as the people attentively heard him, "*Freedom, is not free, freedom is purchased with blood, freedom can only be taken by force. The freedom that we once had is the freedom that we must fight for, freedom will not be handed to us as a free gift, for freedom has a price and that price is death if it's necessary! If you're not willing to die for your freedom then you're already dead, for a man without a choice is dead, the dead can't choose where to be buried, the dead can't choose where to sit nor where to stand; stand is what we will do, and standing we'll remain!*" Barabbas words were electrifying and captivating, there was no one sitting down, everyone was on their feet and chanted, "freedom, freedom, freedom!"

Barabbas continued his speech by saying, "*Not even an ox if it had fallen in a hole would remain there as we have remained in this Roman hole where everyone that passes by shakes theirs head and says, "these people, their God delivered them from the nation of Egypt, was He not able to deliver them from Rome?"* Barabbas shook his fist in the air and the people would ignite in a chant of one voice, "freedom, freedom, freedom!"

Sitting among the crowd was a young man by the name of Peter who was captivated by Barabbas' passion to bring freedom to the people of Israel. Peter also had been waiting for this coming King; Peter was a fisherman from Galilee he had been following Barabbas' movement for some time. He was impressed by the courage and the message of defiance that Barabbas presented. He shared the same feelings Barabbas had about Rome however; he was not fully persuaded especially after hearing about a man named Jesus from Nazareth. The locals went about whispering that Jesus was the new and upcoming so called "*deliverer*".

As Barabbas was bringing his speech to an end he reminded the people by saying, "*My people we must not forget that unless we choose to fight for our land, our nation, our families, then we have already chosen to not be remembered in the history of mankind. By choosing not to fight, we have also chosen to deny our God's existence! Let us not forget our patriarchs, Moses, who delivered the people from Egypt, Gideon, who defended the land with 300 men and won, David, who defended our nation and brought peace to it. It is now our time!*"

That night Peter witnessed the influence of Barabbas. He had seen his people's faith and hope rise to the occasion, but in the back of his mind there was still that name that kept creeping up to his curiosity, "*Jesus the Nazarite*".

THE ASSAULT

That night after his speech, Barabbas headed over to the next town to speak again to the young men for his movement. While he traveled his way, he heard a voice with a Roman accent "*Hey you!" cried out a soldier. Barabbas was defiant and ignored him. The soldier with a more authoritative voice addressed him again, "Hey you... Israelite! Come! Carry my bag!*" Barabbas in his indignation and anger took his time to obey nevertheless he walked towards the soldier. When he got close enough to the soldier, he received a strike to his head by the soldier's rod, he yelled at him, "*I said come! You filthy pig! Carry my bag!!*" Barabbas had the nerve to carry that soldier's bag not one mile, as was the requirement according to the Roman law, but two miles! By doing this he conveyed to the Romans soldier, "*I do what I want and how I want.*"

These types of actions and attitude are what caused Barabbas to gain a credible reputation of being an enemy of the Roman empire. This reputation preceded Barabbas and gave him validity among his followers. These actions brought hope to his following.

Next day in the next town Barabbas called once again for his followers to come to gather at the secret place where they would meet to plan and discuss the future of the movement. Plotting robberies was an element that was never absent during these meetings. The people praised and the applauded loudly over the testimony of how the Roman soldier stood speechless when Barabbas decides

TRUTH?... POSSIBLE?... PERHAPS?

to take his bag two miles that day. "*Long live Barabbas!*" they shouted, and still others shouted, "*Long live Barabbas, our deliverer!*" Their hope was alive, they believed that one day they would overthrow the power of Rome and they would be the nation they used to be. "*Barabbas will give us freedom!*" they chanted. Barabbas quieted the crowd and said, "*Freedom is what all men of Israel want, and freedom is what they will receive, but freedom can't be obtained with rocks! Nor with sticks!*

We need more weapons, more swords for those that have joined themselves to us."

"**James and John,**" called Barabbas "*tomorrow evening a man carrying a bag will come from Jerusalem he is traveling to Jericho, go! You know what you must do.*" James and John were brothers and carried the nick name, Sons of Thunder. Without hesitation, at Barabbas' order, they went on their way. It was a one day's journey, to the place assigned by their leader and waited for their target.

They waited while there was plenty of day light and suddenly, they saw their target! As the target got close enough both of John and James jumped out from where they were hiding. They surprised the man; they beat him and took all of his valuables including a bag he was carrying. They ran off quickly and left him for dead.

After some time, a religious man, a priest of Israel, was passing by the same way and saw the wounded man lying on the street. He looked like a dead man in the middle of the road. As he passed by him, he went around him and continued on his journey. Not soon after another man was passing by and likewise saw the man lying there like a dead man in the middle of the road and also passed him by and continued his journey. Hours had gone by and with the sun almost gone, another traveler came by and

TRUTH?... POSSIBLE?... PERHAPS?

drawing close to him, he could hear a weak moan from the man injured on the road, so he said, "*good man are you alright? What happened to you?*" the man could not respond for he had been beaten close to death all that came out of that man were painful moans.

"*I'm here be of good courage; you're going to be fine.*" He picked him up, put him on his horse, and continued to the closest town. "*Stay with me now, don't let go, soon we will arrive*", said the kind man that picked up the wounded man. When they got close to town there was a water creek, so he got him off his horse and cleaned up the man, bound his wounds, and gave him drink. The wounded man attempting to talk would just moan as if he wanted to know who this man was or to thank him for his kindness, but the man was too weak he had lost a lot of blood and soon he fainted.

Two days later the man woke up to the sound of a rooster outside his window, he didn't know where he was or what day it was. With the little strength he had left he got dressed and noticed that the clothes he put on weren't his clothes! The robe was new and nothing he had purchased; trying to make sense of everything he went out to the lobby of the Inn.

He asked the innkeeper, "*Where am I? How did I get here? How long have I been here?*"

"*You're at the only Inn in town*", replied the Inn Keeper, "*today is Wednesday; you have been here since Monday night*".

"*Who brought me here, how did I get here?*" asked the wounded man.

"*A kind man brought you, and by the way, don't worry about making payment for your stay here, the man paid for your stay and care*", assured the Inn Keeper

"*Who was he, do you know him?*" the wounded man asked.

"*He said if someone asks just to say it was a Nazarite going to Jericho just like you,*" replied the Inn Keeper

"*Yes, but that doesn't tell me who he is; please, tell me who he is!*" shouted the man becoming agitated.

The Inn Keeper waved his hand to calm him down said, "*Sir, if you want to know who he is why don't you go your way, weren't you going to Jericho yourself? I'm sure you'll find him.*"

"*How will I know who he was? How will I find him?*" asked the man.

The Inn keeper replied, "*Well, he said these words, "All men will see me be lifted high*", *I don't really know what he meant by that, but if all men will see him I'm sure you won't miss him*".

The man still pondering on all of what just had taken place, made his way towards Jericho.

TRUTH?... POSSIBLE?... PERHAPS?

THE PREPARATION

As the days of an Israelite festival drew near the Roman government began to make plans for the security of the city. Pilate, who was the governor held his normal meetings right before this particular feast of Israel.

"*As you know that the feast of the Passover is fast approaching us, we need to secure the city,*" Pilate informed his men, "*especially with this Barabbas guy who is a threat to us. Double your security this year, regardless of the cost, the peace of Rome must be kept.*"

Gamaliel responded, "*Your Excellence as I said before concerning Barabbas, he's not a threat to Rome. He talks a good talk among the locals, that's why his name keeps coming up among the people, the one that you should consider and be aware of, is this new and upcoming leader that calls himself the King of the Jews.*" Pilate was frozen by what he heard; he always thought that Cesar was out of his mind when he started the rumor of this baby boy born to be the King of the Jews.

"*Say on*" Pilate replied to Gamaliel, "*tell us of this none sense, I'm sure all of us here will find it amusing, a King of the Jews? Ha!*" Pilate mocked.

Gamaliel proceeded to say, "*Your Excellence, as superstitious as it may sound, Israel is filled with hope. There are rumors that large crowds follow him. This is his account, in the year of Cesar in the city of Bethlehem a baby boy was born to a young couple, the people began to be-*

lieve that this baby boy was their deliverer, your comrade Cesar threatened by his Kingship, put a decree to kill all male boys under two years of age"

"*Get to the point Gamaliel!*" Pilate interrupted, "*or are you also a believer of this deliverer of your people?*"

"*Your Excellence,*" Gamaliel continued, "*whether fairy tale or rumor to you, to the people of Israel it is their living hope, of course not everyone believes that he is the King of the Jews. Some say that he is just another prophet, but what you should know is that his movement is quickly increasing. I'm not a believer, but I am cautious of him, something that your Excellence should consider, and I say this with all due respect.*"

"*Fine, I will look into this matter.*" Pilate responded and quickly assigned undercover people to filter themselves among the local people and to bring back report.

Immediately, his special team of spies descended into town to filter themselves as part of the locals. After three days the spies had come back to give their report to Pilate. Once in the courtyard they began to inform Pilate of their findings, one said, "*I overheard people talking of this Barabbas that Gamaliel seems to be defending, the word is that during this festival day he will try to overthrow Rome*"

Pilate sarcastic laugh interrupted the spy, Pilate asked, "*With what? Sticks?*"

"*No, your Excellence*" replied the spy, "*the rumor is that many people are supporting his plot and they are well armed*".

"*Well he'd better have a good plan,*" Pilate sarcastically laughed. He ordered, "*See to it that we double our security during the days of their feast.*" The spy departed quickly to do just as Pilate had ordered.

TRUTH?... POSSIBLE?... PERHAPS?

Another spy came to Pilate and reported, "*Your Excellence I found what might seem as a deserter from this Jesus of Nazareth, his name is Judas. I found him in the marketplace and lured him into trusting me; his conversation seemed as if he had developed second thoughts about the man he followed or either he was in a mess himself, I also learned Judas has a gambling problem.*"

"*How do you know this?*" Asked Pilate.

"*Well sir, after our conversation I followed him into the local bar in town, without being detected. I witnessed how he gambled money away that he had in his bag. He was losing and pawned his means of transportation to try to win back what he had lost. I left and hurried back to inform your Excellence about this potential link*"

"*Great job, go back and keep an eye on him,*" said Pilate.

Finally, the last spy said, "*Your Excellence I also bring you report. I learned that this Nazirite truly does call himself a King. I was able to locate him, what I found to be odd was his cause. He repeatedly said, "Pray for your enemies, turn the other cheek if they smite you and that his Kingdom was not from this world and that his father was God himself! When he said that God was his father many of the people that followed him stopped following him and went back from where they came from and I made my way back here to report to you.*"

Pilate attentively listened and pondered, trying to understand these sayings; finally, he said, "*Fine. You are dismissed.*"

That night Pilate couldn't sleep. His wife had notice him that evening that he was somewhat troubled and perplexed.She gently asked him, "*Are you alright? What's*

TRUTH?... POSSIBLE?... PERHAPS?

wrong?" Pilate remained troubled but responded, *"Well my spy brought me report of this Nazarite person and I can't figure him out. I don't know what to do about him whether to arrest him or to consider him a lunatic because the things he says are strange".* When Pilate's wife heard this she couldn't hide her surprised look. Pilate asked her, *"Okay...so what does that look on your face mean? What's wrong with you?"*

"Well, you see, last week one of our servants from our kitchen was talking with the kitchen crew how this man you just mentioned heals the sick and even raises the dead. The servant himself did not believe; out of curiosity he located the Nazarite; with his own eyes he saw the miracles that were worked through his hands. He also mentioned that he witnessed some of the chief priest debating with him, so obviously he's not with them nor is he like them. What this servant said, that is alarming, is that this Nazarite claims to be the son of God."

As Pilate listened, he could tell that his wife was holding back on all that she knew, he insisted, *"Tell me what else bothers you!"*

She responded, *"Well, I don't know if I'm bothered by it or confused, since our servant shared these things, I have had dreams about this Nazarite, and I don't even know him! But in my dreams, I can see him, and it is as if he knows me!!"* Pilate's wife began to sob uncontrollably. Pilate embraced and comforted her. He whispered quietly in her ear *"Let's rest and try to get some sleep"*

But Pilate was not at peace. Something was not right in his soul about this man and after several hours he finally fell asleep from exhaustion.

THE PLAN

One month before the feast Barabbas began to provide instructions to his followers on how to carry out the plan to overthrow Rome.

When they were at the place of assembly, Barabbas addressed the crowd by saying, "*As you know the feast of our people draws near. We must prepare with the people here as we've done in other cities; we will meet here every day for the following week to train and practice. The plan of attack is as we've done in the other cities, and when it's time we will all get together and execute our attack - they will not know what hit them*". As usual the people were hopeful and with electrifying chants would fill the air saying, "*Long live Barabbas!*"

Soon enough people were dismissed and early next morning everyone was present, young and old, full of expectancy and their hope more alive than ever. Barabbas and his inner circle quickly got everyone in position and began to train the people on how to better handle a sword; this went on for hours and hours. The people from Galilee were strong, vibrant men. Peter had joined those to be part of this attack, and soon enough he got the handle of swinging a sword it seems he was born to do exactly that.

Barabbas saw Peter's potential and asked, "*What's your name and where are you from?*"

"*My name is Peter and I'm from Galilee*"

TRUTH?... POSSIBLE?... PERHAPS?

"What are you doing here or better yet; do you know what you're doing here?" asked Barabbas.

"I'm part of the hope our people need and yes I know what I'm here for and you can count on me to do what it takes!"

Barabbas liked what he heard coming out of Peter's mouth and said, "*I'm taking you aside for special training I have something in mind for you*"

"*I'm at your disposal; I'll do whatever it takes!*" Peter responded; he was honored to be considered.

After days of training the people were ready, and during this time Barabbas had taken a special liking to Peter. He set him in charge of a group of people; Peter had displayed what Barabbas was looking for, bravery, boldness and over all loyalty till death.

As the day grew closer to overthrow Rome Barabbas was in a good mood and spoke to the crowd one last time before the day of the takeover, he said, "*Finally the day that you and I have been waiting for has drawn near! It has been an honor knowing you and training you for this purpose. My father birthed me to bring deliverance to the people by the people, no longer we will carry Roman bags one mile, no longer we will be a reproach to the nations, no longer will they shake their heads and ask, "couldn't their God that delivered them from Egypt deliver them from Rome?" "Now is the time our people have been waiting for, now is the time we become the nation we were intended to become, today the world would know that our God is alive and well!*" the people full of hope and courage filled the air with a cry of victory, they could taste freedom.

"*Furthermore*" said Barabbas, "*Go into town eat and drink for tomorrow we fight!*" The people were still chee-

TRUTH?... POSSIBLE?... PERHAPS?

ring and chanting Barabbas' name as they dispersed; the crowds of people went into whatever town was closest to their homes. As the night grew old people were eating and drinking and as one knows wine loosens the tongue. A spy sent by Pilate was at the right place and at the right time drinking among some of the young men that had just been with Barabbas. The spy heard the men speaking of the plot to overthrow Rome he made his way quickly back to Pilate.

After traveling all night, the spy finally arrived before Pilate and reported what he heard, "*Your Excellence*" he said, "*I filtered into the next town's bar and I began to drink with four young men. As the evening grew and the wine took its toll one of the young men began to speak of this plot of overthrowing Rome tomorrow during their feast.*"

Pilate immediately ordered for a unit of soldiers and sent them with the spy into the town where the spy had been. Upon arrival they began to ransack the town house by house until they found the men the spy had been drinking with. They began to interrogate them, but they would not speak.

The captain of the unit of soldiers took his sword against one of the young men's neck and motioned to the rest of them to speak or else he would die. "*Who's your captain? Speak you lousy pigs, speak!*" ordered the Roman soldier.

The captain continued to threaten the men to speak but the young man making eye contact with his crew would only shake his head for them to not say anything - in an instant he was dead. The rest of the young men were arrested.

In no time the word of what happened to the men got to Barabbas and he became enraged. He couldn't believe what happened. "*How could they do this? This is non-*

sense, we were so close, why did they have to open their big mouth? My god; now what?!' He was at a loss for what the next step should be.

The next day Barabbas gathered everyone and addressed them. He informed everyone of what had taken place and decided that it was best to cancel the plan until further notice, he preferred that then to have all his men dead and his plan ruined. This news was not received well by the people, nevertheless they trusted their leader, and despite the disappointment they remained hopeful.

Meanwhile Pilate had his assigned soldiers to interrogate those they arrested to get more information out them, specifically the location of their leader Barabbas.

Now Barabbas after dismissing the people stayed behind with his most elite core group and gave them instructions if he should be arrested what they needed to do to keep the cause alive. He was not about to throw away what he had worked so hard for nor did he intend to bring more reproach to the people of Israel.

Barabbas commanded his elite group to go back to their families and stay low until further notice. That day was the longest day of his life. Loneliness set in Barabbas' heart for the very first time since he left his mother's house. Barabbas started to think about her and after much thought he made his way back home.

Barabbas mother was drawing water from the well when she recognized the shadow drawing closer to her, yes, it was her son. Dropping the bucket of water that she had just drawn up, she ran towards him and when she was close enough, she stopped for a moment to admire him. She ran towards him and threw herself on him with her arms wide open.

TRUTH?... POSSIBLE?... PERHAPS?

Barabbas felt unworthy of his mother's love said, "*Mother, I'm not worthy to be called your son, when you needed me the most, I walked out on you.*" Barabbas' mother replied, "*My son was blind but now you see, come and let me feed you, it seems you've been traveling for quite some time now.*" She took the few things he had in his traveling bag and kissed him as if he had never left. The next day when Barabbas woke up, breakfast was waiting at the kitchen table for him. He had missed the aroma of his mother's cooking. While rubbing his eyes and still waking up he made his way to the kitchen and kissed his mother, "*Good morning,*" he said. They began to talk as if nothing ever had happened. But lots of things had happened, they both knew this, but neither wanted to ruin the moment of reconciliation.

As the days went by, Barabbas built up his courage and shared his accomplishments as well as his troubles with his mother. His mother experienced an emotional rollercoaster as he shared all the things that had taken place during his absence.

She responded calmly, trying to not aggravate or worry her son, "*Barabbas, now you know that those Romans soldiers will not stop until they get the truth from those young men, they arrested and next thing they will be after you.*"

Barabbas didn't express fear or disappointment saying, "*I know mom. I just wanted to see you and tell you that love you. I will be leaving first thing tomorrow morning.*"

"*Where will you go?*" Barabbas' mother asked. "*They will find you wherever you go. Why don't you just turn yourself in? It could be that they will spare your life. It could also spare my heart from breaking.*"

"*I can't do that mom,*" Barabbas answered, "*as I said before I will leave first thing tomorrow morning.... I love*

TRUTH?... POSSIBLE?... PERHAPS?

you mom." That night Barabbas couldn't sleep, he spent his time thinking of what would be of everyone. Surrendering was an option that had crossed his mind. However, his pride wouldn't allow him to surrender. He also considered becoming a fugitive, but his pride would not allow him to become someone he wasn't; a coward. After much thought he returned to his original plan to free his people.

Early the next morning Barabbas left a note for his mom and departed with a plan to rob again, as he had done before, and provide for his cause; the overthrow of Rome.

TRUTH?... POSSIBLE?... PERHAPS?

BARABBAS ARRESTED

Barabbas was well aware that the feast days were taking place. He knew that people from all over would be travelling and he saw the opportunity to make some money. This time he would do the job himself. He didn't want to jeopardize the movement he had created.

Meanwhile, more of Barabbas men were arrested and questioned regarding the rumors of overthrowing Rome. However, his comrades would not confess to anything. Barabbas had done a great job training his followers.

After several days of interrogation, Pilot grew weary of not being able to get them to talk. So, he decided to flush Barabbas out. Pilot called on Gamaliel, their informant, and inquired about Barabbas' family. He learned that the only person Barabbas had left was his mother. He quickly assigned a group of his soldiers to bring her to him.

It did not take long for Barabbas to catch wind of what Pilot, the governor of Rome, had ordered. As quickly as he could, Barabbas went back to his mother's house to intercept her arrest. Unfortunately, the Roman soldiers had gotten there before him. Without thinking twice, Barabbas undid his sword and started swinging away attempting to defend his mother. But it was of no use. The Roman soldiers outnumbered him and arrested him.

"*Barabbas! Barabbas!*" his mother cried out, "*It's going to be alright, do not forget that our God will deliver us!*" These were the last words Barabbas heard his mom say

TRUTH?... POSSIBLE?... PERHAPS?

before they took him away and let her go. Those words kept re-sounding in Barabbas' mind. He would grow angrier and angrier, "*How Ironic, the God of our fathers will deliver us! Sure, and so what is he waiting for, for the Romans to ridicule us more? Isn't it enough, when is it enough!? Ahhhhgh*" Those thoughts were repeating over and over in his mind.

Once Pilot found out of Barabbas' arrest, he immediately made his way to the city jail where he would for first time set his eyes on this Barabbas who has been talked about so much.

When Pilot arrived at the city jail Gamaliel, the traitor as the Israelites knew him, was waiting for Pilot with lots of information to share. Gamaliel wore a smirk of satisfaction as if he himself had captured Barabbas.

"*Ahh, dear governor we knew you were coming, therefore, we decided to hurry down here and meet you to inform you that we have Barabbas in the farthest dungeon cell*," said Gamaliel.

Pilot completely disregarded Gamaliel. He walked past him as if he didn't exist. Pilot said, as if to the air, "*Shut up! What is this, "We" stuff? Take me to him immediately and you're dismissed!!*"

Gamaliel and the Romans guards did exactly as Pilot ordered. When they got close to the cell where Barabbas was Pilot said to Gamaliel, "*That's all*!"

Gamaliel wanted to see Barabbas, so he didn't leave as he'd been instructed. Pilot said again, with a firm voice, "*I- said - that is all!*"

Gamaliel left looking like a dog with its ears dropped over his face.

Pilot ordered the guards to open the door to the cell to

demonstrate to Barabbas that he wasn't intimidated. He looked at Barabbas up and down and smirked at him saying, "*So you are the great deliverer of Israel? Ha-ha-ha*" he laughed, "*I'm all ears. Tell me, how were you planning on overthrowing the great Roman Empire? With sticks? Ha-ha-ha.*" He laughed, "*Oh I have it, with brooms to sweep us away with your great army of girls! Ha-ha-ha!*"

Pilot turned to his guards and ordered, " *Bring me those kids that gave this piece of trash up!*" Quickly the guards went to the general population cell block and brought the young men. Pilot said to Barabbas, "*Here is your great army, you should have seen and heard them squawking like little girls and now we are here all together, ha-ha-ha-ha.*"

Barabbas knew that his men were loyal and would never say anything to betray him. He also knew that Pilot, the Governor, had served in the armed forces of Rome. Therefore, he was very strategic. He knew that a kingdom divided against itself could not succeed. Pilot was trying to bring division between the men and Barabbas.

Barabbas spoke with wisdom, "*with all due respect, if my people are a laughingstock to you, then release them. You got me. I'm the one you wanted.*"

Pilot exploded with anger and practically growled saying, "*I sure got you, didn't I? Don't you ever tell me what to do, you hear me!? To prove to you that this is a laughing matter I will let them go.*"

Pilot called out and ordered, "*Guards bring me female dresses now!*" After a few minutes the guards appeared with ladies' dresses as Pilot had requested. Pilot ordered the soldiers, "*Throw them on the floor. And you "ladies" put them on if you want to leave this place.*"

For a minute the men refused to be made a public spectacle. However, Barabbas ordered them and said, "*Boys, do as he says.*" So, they did. Then they were transported to the middle of the marketplace with a soldier announcing in a loud voice, "*Hear ye, hear ye, this is the army of the great deliverer, Barabbas. Barabbas is now under arrest in our city jail. Let it be made known to all, that anyone who is found following this so called "great" Barabbas will join these little girls in their dresses!*" It was the most humiliating thing that Barabbas' men had ever experienced. This exhibition broke future plans that Barabbas had worked so hard to put together.

When Peter heard of Barabbas' capture and of the humiliation his men went through, he became greatly discouraged. For you see, Peter looked up to Barabbas as the deliverer of Israel. When plans didn't develop as Peter had wanted, his hope began to dissipate.

Peter sat under a tree trying to make sense of all of this. He closed his eyes and when he least expected he had fallen asleep. After a few hours Peter woke up and headed to the seashore to fish, hoping that by working hard he would become distracted from the emotional rollercoaster. By the time he reached the seashore the day was almost over, but it was not too late for fishing. Some of his best catches were done at night. Upon his arrival to where his boats were docked, he gathered his crew and launched out to sea. Peter continued to ponder on the arrest of Barabbas, who was thought of as the Living Hope. It was impossible to accept that the Living Hope, the Light of Israel, was being turned off and coming to an end. Peter decided to take a break from fishing. He directed his crew to continue without him.

Peter made his way to the back of the boat and sat with his head resting on his knees and his hands over his head as if he wanted to disappear. He began to pray to the

TRUTH?... POSSIBLE?... PERHAPS?

God of Israel, "*God of Abraham, Isaac, and Jacob*", Peter continued, "*Never leave us nor forsake us. Remember the promise you made to our fathers of sending a deliverer and setting us free from bondage. Behold Barabbas, the hope of Israel, is now turned off as a candle in the wind, this Barabbas whom you had sent is now no more, I call on you and ask you to rekindle the light of Israel once again*" It was the only prayer that Peter was able to mumble out and then he became silent as discouragement set in.

After an hour away from his crew he returned to them and called unto them, "*So how are we doing? I don't hear any noise. Is everyone asleep?*"

"*No sir*", cried out one of the men, "*There is nothing and pretty soon the sun will be rising. What do you suggest?*" One of the crewmen answered, "*Let's keep throwing those nets out there again. We don't want to return empty handed,*" said Peter. After a couple of hours and with no success, Peter instructed his crew to bring in the nets and head back to shore. When they got into shore the day began to break, and Peter and his crew began the hardest chore in fishing. Yup, cleaning those nets! It was dirty, smelly and difficult work. The chore was more difficult when the fisherman came up empty without a catch.

After a few hours, as they were just about done with the clean-up, Peter glanced up and saw a crowd of people that were coming towards his direction. As the crowd got closer, he was able to recognize the person the crowd was following. It was the man they called Jesus of Nazareth. When Jesus got closer to where Peter was working, the crowd had increased by the people who lived by the shore. Everyone wanted to see and hear the person named Jesus. Jesus called on Peter saying, "Friend, would you allow me to step onto your boat, and speak to this crowd of people? Before they step over me." Peter answered, "*Yes, be my guest!*" Jesus stepped onto Peter's boat and began to teach and speak to the crowd about the Kingdom. However, his message of a new and upcoming Kingdom was different from what Peter had heard Barabbas speak.

When Jesus finished speaking, he sent the crowd away. Then, he told Peter to launch his boat into the deep water for a catch. Peter was reluctant at first because he had just finished washing his nets and was ready to go home! "*What did this preacher man know about fishing?*" he thought to himself. However, he did as Jesus instructed.

Jesus joined them as they went out to sea. To Peter's amazement the catch was so great that he instantly repented and told Jesus, "*Sir, forgive me, I was wrong in thinking that the order you gave me about returning to sea, and throwing my nets again was a total mistake! I see that God is with you*".

When they got to shore Jesus said to Peter, "*Come and follow me and I will make you a fisher of men.*" Peter did not hesitate. He followed Jesus immediately. What he had seen and heard from Jesus renewed a glimmer of the hope he had lost when Barabbas was arrested. The arrest of Barabbas had extinguished the light of hope to those who at one time had followed him. Everyone had dispersed and was keeping a low profile while things cooled down. Peter, now following Jesus, was excited again about Israel becoming a nation. He was especially encouraged when crowds would gather to hear Jesus, who he now followed, "*Jesus the Nazarene*".

TRUTH?... POSSIBLE?... PERHAPS?

THE ELITE

As the fame of the Nazarene grew so did the crowds that followed and once more, the Romans were concerned of this new leader of the Israelites. They were also somewhat confused because this Jesus guy didn't hide or cause any disruptions among the people. The Romans did not know what to think of him. Instead of creating violence he created peace, and instead of proclaiming war he proclaimed love. The Romans were not threatened by him because Jesus was a religious leader and the Romans controlled the religious leaders. Thanks to Gamaliel and other religious groups they worked with.

As time passed. the Barabbas movement was dwindling down more and more. The movement lost momentum and strength; only a few faithful remained. The group sent a woman to visit Barabbas in prison. She informed him about the condition of his followers. The woman would bring Barabbas food to the prison. She was discreet so that his followers would not put themselves in danger of also being arrested.

During a visit, Barabbas received news that crowds of people followed Jesus of Nazareth. Even some of those who at one time were handpicked by Barabbas himself. Men like Peter, James and John. Barabbas was confused and full of anger because of what he heard. Barabbas' anger was due to his people abandoning him. He was also confused because some of the remarks Jesus spoke were: "*My Kingdom is not from this world.*" Also, "*I am sent to the lost people of Israel to save them."* Such declarations would bring some hope to Barabbas. He thought maybe this Jesus will be his ally and could somehow recruit everyone once again and overthrow the Romans. Barabbas did not know what to think about this Jesus guy.

As the months passed by, Jesus' fame increased greatly to the point that he asked those who he had helped to not say who helped them. There were times now that he couldn't even enter a town because people would press on him to the degree that he couldn't walk freely.

On one occasion the crowd was so large that he couldn't walk freely. Jesus was pressed from every side. Suddenly, Jesus asked, "*Who touched me?*" Peter answered, "*Sir with all due respect, everyone is touching you and pressing against us. What do you mean who touched me? Don't you see that everyone is touching you and us?*" Jesus replied, "*Someone touched me.*" A lady, who couldn't hide any longer, drew closer and crying said, "*Sir I touched you! I touched you because I heard of how people have been healed from their infirmities, if they just touch you. I had an infirmity for twelve years and I've gone to many doctors but didn't get any better. The infirmity became worse. And on top of that, I ran out of money. When I heard about you, I quickly came to see you. I knew that if I can touch even the hem of your garment I would be made well, and I did, I did get well!! Sir, you were my only hope, and what they said about you was true! I'm healed!! I kept saying to myself if I just get a chance to touch the hem of his garment, just like the other people did, I also will get healed and I did!!!*" The woman couldn't stop weeping. Jesus responded to her, "*Daughter, your faith has made you well.*"

When Peter saw and heard this, he was embarrassed of the response he gave Jesus when he said someone touched him. Once again, his impulsiveness had gotten him to speak foolishness. After many incidents like the woman who was healed, Jesus decided to organize the crowds. He would gather them in groups of one hundred and other times in groups of fifty; he was able to speak to them and attend to their needs. He also selected seventy men to train and empower to go before him and spread the message that he carried which was, "*Repent for the Kingdom of God is at hand.*" One of the times the seventy returned from their mission. They were excited about the great exploits God had done through them. Jesus told them, "*Do not be happy because of the results you're getting in my name but be happy that your names are written in the book of life*". Within the seventy men Jesus hand pick twelve of whom he called apostles, which means "*the sent ones.*" For he would send them, and they would declare the Kingdom of God. They also tended to the people's needs just as Jesus would.

Jesus was going to Jerusalem with the apostles. Jesus took the twelve aside again and began to tell them the things that would happen, "*Behold, we are going up to Jerusalem, and the Son of Man will be betrayed to the chief priests and to the scribes; and they will condemn Him to death and deliver Him to the Gentiles; and they will mock Him, and scourge Him, and spit on Him, and kill Him. And on the third day He will rise again.*" The apostles were clueless about what they just heard. Often time Jesus would say things that they were not always sure what he meant.

James and John, the sons of thunder as they were known, came to Jesus, saying, "*Teacher, we want you to do for us whatever we ask.*" and he said to them, "*What do you want me to do for you?*" They said to him, "*Grant us that we may sit, one on your right hand and the other on your left, once you establish your Kingdom*"

But Jesus said to them, "*You do not know what you ask.*

Are you able to drink from the cup that I drink, and be baptized with the baptism that I am baptized with?"

They said to him, "*we are able.*" Jesus said to them, "*You will indeed drink the from cup that I drink. And with the baptism I am baptized you will be baptized. But to sit by my right hand and by my left is not mine to give, but it is for those for whom it is prepared."*

When the other apostles heard about James and John's request, they began to be greatly displeased with James and John. Jesus called them to himself and said to them, "*You know that those who are considered rulers over the Gentiles lord it over them and exercise authority over them. Yet, it shall not be so among you. Whoever desires to become great among you shall be your servant, and whoever of you desires to be first shall be servant of all. For even the Son of Man did not come to be served, but to serve, and to give His life as ransom for many."*

Once again, the apostles were clueless of what he said to them, the only thing that kept them believing in him were his deeds and the crowds that followed him.

This newfound leader, Jesus of Nazareth, was so different from Barabbas. Nevertheless, he brought some concern to the Romans. They never considered Jesus a threat, although they knew that the threat was towards the religious groups. The religious groups were jealous of how many people followed Jesus; they sought to kill him. These religious leaders were burning with hate when they heard that crowds followed Jesus and his apostles. Also, how through the hands of the apostles many signs and wonders were done among the people. The people esteemed Jesus and the apostles highly. Believers, both men and women, were increasingly added to the movement Jesus had created.

BARABBAS AND JOHN MEET

When the religious leaders heard of Jesus' popularity growing, they were furious and plotted to kill him. Then Gamaliel stood up. Being a part of the largest religious group, the Pharisees, Gamaliel was one of the most influential teachers of the law and he was held in respect. Gamaliel continued to say to those who sought to kill Jesus *"Men of Israel, take heed, what you intend to do regarding this man. For some time ago Theudas rose up, claiming to be somebody. A number of men, about four hundred, joined him. He was killed, and all who obeyed him were scattered and came to nothing. After this man, Judas of Galilee rose up in the days of the census and drew many people after him. He also perished, and all who obeyed him were dispersed. And now I say to you, keep away from these men and let them alone; for if this plan or this work is of men, it will come to nothing; but if it is of God, you cannot overthrow it—lest you even be found to fight against God."* And they agreed with Gamaliel.

It had been close to two years that Barabbas had been in prison. He had grown bitter at life and angrier at the one Israel called God. Those that at one time visited him came less and less. One day while in his cell he heard the door of the hallway open, so he got close. Pressed against the bars of his cell, he heard and saw Roman soldiers bringing in a new prisoner. The soldiers pushed and shoved him into the cell next to him. Barabbas lost his composure and started to curse and scream at the soldiers saying, "*leave*

TRUTH?... POSSIBLE?... PERHAPS?

him alone, enough of that, he's already handcuffed what danger is he to you? Enough of that!" The soldiers ignored Barabbas, closed the cell door behind the new prisoner, and walked out of the prison block. Barabbas curious of who his new neighbor was and at the same time in much need of some company asked, " *Hey, who are you? what are you here for?*" In a hurting broken voice, that had just been beaten by the Romans soldier, the voice answered, " *I am John. People call me John the Baptist* ".

John asked, "*what about you, who are you and what are you in here for?*"

Barabbas introduced himself and spent much of the day sharing his story until the night grew old.

The next day when the Romans soldiers began to feed the prisoners, Barabbas checked on his new cellblock neighbor. He called out, "*Hey John are you awake? How are you doing? Come on and get up. You need to stand by your cell door, or you won't be eating this morning*" Barabbas could hear John waking up, still moaning from the beating he had received. John quickly approached the door cell to receive his ration of food. When the soldiers left John asked Barabbas, "*what kind of food is this? Do they expect us to eat this?*"

Barabbas said, " *You better get used to it quick or you'll end up starving*". With a face of disgust John started to eat what they brought him. Although, he wasn't able to keep it down. He quickly vomited as soon as he finished his plate.

"*Ha-ha-ha! What happen John having trouble over there?*" Barabbas asked.

"*I don't know how you can eat this mess*" John answered,

"*Well, welcome to the best Inn in town ha-ha-ha-ha-ha,*" Barabbas laughed.

TRUTH?... POSSIBLE?... PERHAPS?

John, being new in the cell block, continued to inquire about the living conditions. Barabbas explained to John that unless inmates had any visits from friends or family, prison food was the only option.

"*What about you?*" John asked, "*Do you have any visitors?*"

Barabbas took a moment before answering and said, "*when I first arrived none came. They were afraid of the Roman soldiers arresting them just for knowing me. After a few months, I had a small group of my followers that would come once a week to visit me and bring me food, and provide me with news about the condition of the revolutionary movement that I led*"

"*Revolutionary movement?*" John asked

"*Yes.*" Barabbas responded. Barabbas spent the next several hours talking to John about his cause and why he was there.

After hours of John attentively listening to Barabbas, he wasn't sure of what to say or if it was a good idea to say anything at all. It was very clear who Barabbas was and what he stood for.

"*Well enough about me,* "said Barabbas. "*Even though it felt good to talk to someone else other than to myself. I haven't been able to talk to anyone since I got here.*"

John broke his silence and answered, "*Why is this cell block almost empty? Out of the 10 cells here there are but a few of us here*".

Barabbas said, "*this cell block is for murderers only.*" John almost fainted and exclaimed, "*What! I'm not a murderer. Why did they bring me here?! I can't believe it, what are they thinking, this is outrages, I didn't murder anyone!*" John went on and on.

TRUTH?... POSSIBLE?... PERHAPS?

Finally, Barabbas responded loudly to him *"Shut up John! Get a hold of yourself. You're here now so just shut up!"* John quickly came to himself. Barabbas said, *"I'll talk to you later. Enough for now. You got me in a bad mood with your complaining"*.

Barabbas lay on his bunk bed made from concrete and gazed up at the moist cold ceiling in his cell. He began to reminisce about how far he had gotten with his cause and although he had disappointment and anger towards the God of his father's. He, for the very first time in a long time, began to have an inward dialog with God. "So where are you God? Why do you abandon your people? Weren't you the God that opened the red sea for them and drowned the Pharaoh and his army? Why can't you deliver us now? Are you asleep? Why don't you answer me?" This was the inward dialogue that Barabbas had with God but there was no answer. Only silence.

TRUTH?... POSSIBLE?... PERHAPS?

DIMAS AND GESTAS THE TWO THIEVES

Barabbas woke to the sound of screams and shouts. He quickly arose and got close to his cell door to see two more prisoners brought in and quickly shoved into their own cells. Barabbas called on John to come close to his own cell door, "*John, John are you awake?*" Barabbas spoke under his breath as the Romans soldiers exited the cell block.

John answered, "*Yes, I'm awake. Who can sleep or even think with all this noise around here?*"

Barabbas said, "*It looks like we have some more company. They just brought two more prisoners; I wonder what they did.*"

John answered, "*I don't know and at this moment I don't really care*"

Barabbas said, "*well then tell me more about you. Tell me what you are in here for. Who exactly are you? Earlier I told you almost everything about myself*".

John answer "*yea...I wish you wouldn't have done that. I don't want them to think that I'm with your movement the one you spoke so proudly about. Describing to me what you guys did and stood for*"

Barabbas quickly said, "*Oh please John. What are they going to do? Take you to jail? You're already in jail so get over it and tell me why you are in here for?*"

After a few moments of silence John decided to share

TRUTH?... POSSIBLE?... PERHAPS?

with Barabbas his present situation. John started by saying, "*well, as I said before I'm not a murderer, and I don't know why they put me in this particular cell block*"

Barabbas interrupted, "*you told me that already. If that is true then you must have done something really bad, my friend! What did you do?*"

John continued to tell Barabbas, "*Well, you see, I'm a preacher*"

Barabbas interrupted, "*a preacher, a, preacher? You got to be kidding me! What is a preacher doing here with us murderers? Ha-ha-ha*"

John responded, "*Well you see I'm not only a preacher, but God sent me to prepare the way for the deliverer of Israel*"

Barabbas interrupted again, "*oh no. Here we go, don't tell me them fairytales again. I heard all of them and everything is a lie. Look at you now. If that's true that the deliverer of Israel is coming and you are supposed to work for him, why are you here? Please save it for another day.*"

John said, "*what's wrong? Don't you believe? Why did you get like that? Did I say something that upset you?*"

Barabbas answered back with anger, "*If that God or that King of Israel that is supposed to come to deliver us is so real why doesn't he do something about it? Why are the Romans oppressing his people? Look at us we are both here, come on John get a hold of yourself, wake up those are just legends that we've been hearing for years*"

This time, John interrupted Barabbas and said, "*I'm sorry you feel that way about what I'm telling you but it is true, let me finish telling you why I got arrested, and stop interrupting me or do you want me to stop?*"

TRUTH?... POSSIBLE?... PERHAPS?

Barabbas said, "*No of course not, go ahead continue*"

John continued with his story, but he never forgot the response and the reaction of Barabbas.

John said, "*Well as I was telling you I'm a preacher and I had been telling Herod the King of Judea that what he was doing with his brother Philip's former wife was against Gods law. When I preached to the crowds of people, I would mention it to them as part of my sermon, to turn from your sins, so he had me arrested. Before they put me in here, Herod had me before him and told me that what I was doing was not acceptable and can cause an uproar or a revolution because of his image being slandered, and that he had to do what he had to do, so he put me here with you all. Now I'm here and I can't understand why they put me in this section of this prison it's not like I killed someone*"

Barabbas responded, "*Well maybe you should talk to your God the one you say is sending his King to deliver us*"

John did not respond to Barabbas' comment, which confused him and caused doubt to cross John's mind.

"*Why so quiet now John?*" Barabbas asked, "*Doesn't it make sense? Look we are both here in prison and there is none coming to save us, you can't possibly believe that there is a deliverer coming! I at one time believed that I could become that deliverer that Israel needed. All it got me was this cell.*"

John said, "*I don't know Barabbas, I just don't know, I'll talk to you later.*" John went to lie down and pondered at Barabbas' words.

After that conversation with John, Barabbas yelled out across the prison hall, "*Hey! Hey, you guys, who are you and what are you in for?*"

TRUTH?... POSSIBLE?... PERHAPS?

The two new prisoners drew close to their door cell and one of them said, "*I'm Dimas*" and the other also said, "*I'm Gestas.*" Barabbas introduced himself by saying, "*I'm, Barabbas*".

Dimas and Gestas began speaking over each other saying, "*Oh yea, we heard about you and your movement! That was quite a run you gave the Romans. Hey, look at it this way you gave it your all my friend*".

Barabbas interrupted and asked again, "*What are you here for?*"

Gestas answered, "*They caught us stealing a Roman shipment of goods.*"

"*Yea, but if it wasn't for you and your lack of patience our plan would have worked out. If we just waited for the sun to go down.*" Dimas added angrily. Gestas defended himself saying, "*Shut up! It was a good plan*"

Barabbas asked, "*Why are you here in this part of the prison? This side is exclusively for murderers.*" John yelled from his cell, "*no its not, I'm not one of them, I'm here for telling the truth!*"

Gestas responded to Barabbas, "*The prison is overpopulated so they put us here*".

Barabbas yelled, "*See John, now you can rest at peace with your 'Why am I here?' whining. It doesn't matter. A prison cell is a prison cell*"

Dimas one of the thieves said, "*We overheard your partner say he was a preacher and that he was here to tell the truth, ha-ha-ha.*" He laughed, "*Maybe you should have lied like some of the other religious leaders, and you would have been out there with them thieves. Because that's what they are, they are bigger thieves than us!*"

TRUTH?... POSSIBLE?... PERHAPS?

Barabbas said, "*See John, what did I tell you? The God of our fathers is asleep, or he doesn't care. Just give it up. No one is coming and you're here with us. So, you're as guilty as we are.*"

John responded, "*I'm guilty alright, but of speaking the truth to Herod*".

Suddenly, their chatting came to an end because the hallway door was opened by the guards who fed the prisoners. They were passing out their only meal for the day.

After they ate, Dimas and Gestas were intrigued about a preacher being in jail and once again they sparked up the conversation with John. Dimas and Gestas got up close to the bars and Dimas screamed out, *"Hey John! I mean, Preacher. So, you mean to tell us that you're here for preaching the truth? What is truth?"*

John replied, "*Truth is repenting from your crooked ways and to be baptized. And believe in him whom I have prepared the way for, his name is Jesus of Nazareth.*" And with many more words did John answer them. After a while Getas said, "*Ok enough preacher man. If that's truth why is it that the King of the Jews, as you proclaim him to be, doesn't save you? You're here with us criminals*"

John said, "*I can't answer that question now, but the time will come for me to answer you and Barabbas as well. Because he also asked me the same question.*". John decided to call it day, by saying to them, "*I'm done for now, I'll talk you guys at another time.*" John went to his bunk bed that night with bother in his mind. It was the questions that he couldn't answer that caused him to doubt at times.

As time passed, Jesus of Nazareth's fame increased to the point that everyone in the prison knew about all that Jesus went about doing.

TRUTH?... POSSIBLE?... PERHAPS?

One day Barabbas asked John, "*Hey preacher, are you awake? Come up to your door let me talk to you.*"

John answered him, "*Yes, I'm up what's going on?*"

Barabbas stared out, "*You know John there was a time when I thought that the God of Israel was real. But the more I saw the suffering of our people the less I believed. It has been almost two years and those who called me friend have stopped visiting me. Soon it will happen to you also*"

John asked, "*What do you mean?*"

Barabbas said, "*I don't know if you knew but my real name is Jesus Barabbas. At one time I believed that the God of Israel had chosen me to deliver his people from the Romans. I don't believe that anymore. Look where we are, you said, you were a preacher who prepares the way for the deliverer of Israel. Did you see him, and did you talk to him? Tell me, what makes you still believe that this Jesus of Nazareth is not just like me? I had people follow me and believing in me, but now as a prisoner they forgot about me just like God forgot about me. I mean if there is even a God, as you preach*"

John answered, "*Yes. I saw him, and yes, I talked to him and baptized him. But, no, I didn't ask what his plan was or how he was going to deliver Israel. You said your full name is Jesus Barabbas? You know what your name means, right?*"

Barabbas answered, "*Well yes, it means the son of the father, the deliverer. That's why I believed that maybe, just maybe, I was to deliver Israel. But now Israel has forgotten their once hero just like God has forgotten me. You know what John? He has forgotten you, too.*"

Those words dug deep into John's heart and for a moment caused him to doubt his faith. The next time John received visitors, he instructed them to ask Jesus whether he was the one that was to come, or should we wait for another.

When the visitors returned to see John, they told him, *"Sir we did as you asked." John replied, "And what did he say? Give me details!"*

They answered, *"Jesus looked at us and almost ignored our question. He was laying his hands on those that were sick and even on those who were blind and they were made well, then after a while he came back to us and said,* " *"Go and tell John the things you have seen: that the blind see, the lame walk, the lepers are cleansed, the deaf hear, the dead are raised, the poor have the gospel preached to them, and blessed is he who is not offended because of Me."*

John was teary eyed. Those who gave him the news did not know whether they were tears of joy or tears of sadness. Either way it was uncomfortable to witness their teacher emotionally moved. John was a man who would stand up to religious leaders and anyone who had ulterior motives. This man was known to pull no punches and display courage like no one else. It was the reason why John was in jail now. John was silent for what seemed hours. He composed himself and changed the topic of conversation. When visiting hours were over John to return to his cell and sobbed silently. They were tears of repentance because for a moment he had allowed his faith to waiver.

TRUTH?... POSSIBLE?... PERHAPS?

JOHN THE PREACHER AND HIS DEATH

Next morning Barabbas called to John, "*Hey John, how are you doing? How was your visit? How are things in town?*"

John got up from his bunk bed with a new fight in his heart. As he approached the cell gate, he began preaching about the deliverer of Israel. John had found a second wind. He preached as he did as a free man outside the prison as he did inside the cell block where Herod had put him in for speaking the truth. John made it a habit of preaching every day from his cell block. Initially, Barabbas was aggravated and displeased that he couldn't silence John. However, the prisoners had no choice but to hear John's message and his bid to repentance. John preached for months, Barabbas and the other prisoners began to change their demeanor.

They began to ask questions about this deliverer of Israel and would ask John, "*Hey John, what's the word of the day?*" John would gladly get close to his cell gate and preach. After months of preaching, John earned the nickname, "*the preacher.*" Some would refer to him as the *"preacher"* because they had believed in their hearts that he spoke the truth. Others would refer to him as "*crazy preacher*" mockingly. Either way, John carried the nick name well. The prisoners who mocked John regarded him as entertainment to keep their minds occupied in prison. For those who believed, John kept their hope alive. Although one is forgotten in prison by the outside world, hope is the only thing that keeps a person alive. John's recharged faith changed the environment of the prison. There was less tension and anger between the prisoners. Even the Roman guards appeared to be friendlier with the prisoners and several of the guards had taken a liking to John. At times the guards would give him sweets and snacks from the outside world. John, in return, would share the treats with those in his cell block. One day John received news that Herod was having a party for his stepdaughter's birthday. Very important people would be attending. This information did not mean much to John. Barabbas, however, realized that a large party is great opportunity to slaughter the Romans in a surprise attack. Although, the idea of attacking was disheartening to Barabbas.

"*How I would have loved to be with my elite crew and slaughter them all while they were all together in one place,*" Barabbas commented.

Gestas agreed with Barabbas and said, "*I wouldn't mind being there to see it and perhaps doing it myself! I'd love to be the one running the knife through their throats.*"

John heard them and said, "*Vengeance is mine sayeth the Lord.*"

Both Barabbas and Gestas started mocking John for saying that, "*Well, it seems that your God is sleeping, because he is taking too long to do that or maybe your God is still thinking about it.*"

Gestas questioned John, "*How can you say that John? How can you believe that? Can't you see how long it's been and where we are? I don't think you're right this time John.*"

John took that opportunity to get against his door cell and preach about love and forgiveness at the top of his voice he spoke with conviction and authority so much that after an hour had passed and he finished speaking. No one said a word, there was a deafening silence.

At the end of the day the doors of the corridor opened, and two Romans soldiers walked in. They were not coming to serve a meal or to pick up the meal plates, they went straight to the cell gate of John and ordered, "*Get up John, you're coming with us.*"

Everyone on the cell block knew this was not a visit, because visiting hours where closed. They all started to yell out "*Where are you taking him? Hey, what's going on? Hey, you can't do that!!*" But the Romans soldiers quickly escorted John out. Little did they know that Herod ordered for John to be taken.

John asked them, "*Where are you taking me? Where am I going? Aren't you going to answer me?*" One of the soldiers said, "*We're just following orders to take you to our ranking officer, you can ask him.*" The Roman guards proceeded to take John through the corridors of the prison until they got to their ranking officer and turned John over to him. The look on the ranking officer's face did not convey good news to the prison guards but they dared not ask a question. They delivered John and returned to their assigned post without a word. The ranking officer proceeded to take John to what seemed to be an inner cell in an isolated area on the bottom floor of the prison; the dungeon.

When John figured out where they were taking him, his life flashed before his eyes. He remembered his parents telling him of his birth and that he was a miracle. He also remembered angel's foretelling of his purpose in life, and how he was to be a voice and prepare the way for the deliverer of Israel. More vivid was his experience at the Jordan River when he heard the thundering voice of God after Jesus came out of the water, declaring, "*this is my beloved son in whom I'm well pleased.*" John's course in life started to fall in place and make sense to him at that moment.

As he was taken into the inner cell of the dungeon and turned over to the executioner, John began to sing hymns to his God. The executioner ordered him to be quiet, but John only sang louder. John was known in the prison as "*the preacher*" and to the outside world as John the Baptist, was to be beheaded.

That night the executioner couldn't sleep. John wasn't the first prisoner he had beheaded during his military career. However, he knew that this execution had been different. He had never witnessed someone singing hymns of joy before their execution. That marked his life forever. His wife asked him, "*What's wrong? you seem troubled.*" He answered, "*As my wife you know the type of work I'm ordered to carry out.*" The wife replied, "*Yes, I do. But it didn't bother you before.*" "*You're right,*" he said "*but this man sung right before his execution about joy and love. When the time came for him to lay his head on the wood stump, he did it willingly almost running to the stump. Normally, I have to push others onto it and hold them down. He also asked me a question.*"

"*What question?*" Asked his wife,

"*Well, he asked if I knew Jesus of Nazareth, the King of the Jews. I did not know what he meant by that so, I proceeded to follow my orders.*"

His wife said, "*I heard that name before in the marketplace. People have different opinions; some say he is a prophet other say he is Elijah still other say he is John the Baptist.*" When the executioner heard that he said, "No, it can't be John the Baptist because John the Baptist is

TRUTH?... POSSIBLE?... PERHAPS?

the man I executed", His wife did not respond. They both stood silence.

The next day the news of John's execution spread through the prison. When the news got to Barabbas and the cell block where John lived, no one knew what to say. Their silence was deafening. Barabbas called out from his cell door to Dimas and Gestas, "*Hey you guys, have you heard that our preacher friend was beheaded last night by order of Herod?*"

Gestas cold heartedly answered, "*What do you mean 'our' friend Barabbas? Are you getting soft on me, now? Ha-ha-ha.*"

Barabbas composing himself said, "*You know what I mean, our cell block mate was beheaded by order of Herod.*" Dimas replied, "Yes. We did. It made me wonder if we're next."

And Gestas said, "*You too, Dimas? Don't tell me he converted both of you? And no. We are not next. We didn't kill anyone to deserve being beheaded. We are just thieves,*"

Dimas said, "*John didn't kill anyone, either. He just told Herod the truth.*"

Gestas said, "*Well he might not have killed anyone, but he sure killed the pride and image of Herod by calling him an adulterer in front of people*". Time went by and the cell block where John had been imprisoned was never the same; at times Dimas would say, "*Don't you guys miss John? I'm almost convinced that everything he said about the deliverer of Israel is true.*"

"*Shut up. What I miss is being entertained by his fairytales,*" said Gestas.

Barabbas replied roughly, "*Shut up, both of you! I'll tell*

TRUTH?... POSSIBLE?... PERHAPS?

you one thing John died as a brave man, he could have always apologized publicly and said that he was wrong. Perhaps Herod would have set him free. He was here, with us in prison, like a prisoner not taking back what he had said about Herod, John died on his feet like a warrior".

Both Dimas and Gestas kept silent.

JESUS ARRESTED

Those who once walked with John went to the authorities to claim John's body; they wanted to give him a proper burial. The news about John's execution reached Jesus. Jesus travelled to a remote area to be alone. However, his fame didn't allow his desire for solitude. As soon as someone discovered his whereabouts, the crowds went to him. When he saw that he couldn't hide, he began to preach asking, "*When you went to John's baptism what did you go to see? A reed swayed by the wind? Or a man dressed in fine clothes? I tell you no, for those that dress in fine linen are in palaces. I tell you what you saw was a prophet. More than that, it was him who was sent before me to prepare the way, truly I tell you among those that are born of woman there is none greater than John*"

Those that brought Jesus the news about John were present and heard how their leader was honored by Jesus.

Afterward Jesus went to the temple with his twelve disciples. He saw from a distance people buying and selling. He leaned against a willow tree and thought about what to do. Jesus cut some of the branches from the willow tree and began to make a whip while meditating the writings of God, "*My house should be called a house a prayer.*".

Jesus entered the temple with his disciples. Suddenly, without giving notice to his disciples, Jesus overturned the tables of the money changers and the merchants inside the temple! Jesus swung the whip at them, causing them to run away. Jesus shouted and swung the whip at the money changers and vendors saying, "*It is written, my house is to be called a house of prayer, but you have turned it into a den of thieves!*"

One of his disciples, Judas Iscariot, did not agree in his heart with what Jesus did that day.

News of Jesus at the temple quickly spread to the religious leaders of the synagogue. The religious leaders of that day did not like Jesus; they were jealous of the large crowds that followed him. His leadership style did not sit well with them. Jesus constantly broke their traditions. However, because the people believed in his message and were in awe of his miracles the religious leaders would not dare touch him. Secretly, a group of them found a weak link among Jesus' disciples. Yes, you guessed it right. Judas Iscariot!

A few days later they went to his house by night. Judas heard a knock at his door and wondered who it could be at this time of night. Judas cracked the door open to see who was there, but he couldn't ignore them because their eyes met. One of the religious leaders served as the spokesman of the group. He asked, "*May we come in?*" His name was Saul

Judas responded with a shaky voice, "*Sure come in. What can I do for you gentleman?*" Saul introduce himself, "*I'm Saul of Tarsus and these are my associates. We belong to the Pharisees. We heard about your leader, Jesus, and the episode he caused at the temple.*" Saul paused and said, "*Excuse my rudeness. Your name sir?*" Judas clearing his throat answered "*Judas. Judas Iscariot.*" Saul proceeded, "*Well Judas, your teacher caused a big scene and we are very concerned. We would like to know your thoughts on what he did at the temple. You were there we-*

TRUTH?... POSSIBLE?... PERHAPS?

ren't you?" Clearing his throat, Judas replied, "*Sir please sit down. May I offer you gentleman something to drink?*" The Pharisees, staring intently, only shook their heads "no." Judas proceeded to answer Saul's question, "*Yes, I was there. But I had no idea that he was going to do what he did. I'm really sorry for that.*" Saul stood silent for what seemed a long time. "*Well Judas, you know that what you guys did carries a huge penalty.*" Judas interrupted Saul, "*Sir, I was there but I did not participate. I was disturbed by Jesus' behavior, just like yourself.*"

Saul continued with his threatening voice, "*Well, I hear what you're saying but you were there. We've spoken with the Roman authority and they also agree that it is enough to put you and your group in jail.*" Judas interrupted, "*Sir, it's not my group. Jesus is our teacher it is he that we follow.*"

Saul said, "*I see that. Nevertheless, you were part of that disorder. What do you think we should do to you?*" Judas answered cowardly, "*Well, I'm willing to make it up to you. If I damaged something in the temple, I'll pay for it.*"

Saul asked, "*Are you trying to bribe us?*" Judas quickly became defensive because of his fear, "*No, sir. No bribes here. Tell me, what can I do to make it right?*"

Saul said, "*Well it's not what you can do for us, but what we can do for you. This crime you were involved in can get you years in a Roman prison. I'll tell you what. We're going to pretend nothing happened. Furthermore, we're going to give you 30 pieces of silver. But you need to help us arrest Jesus. No one else is going to get hurt or go to jail. What do you say?*"

Judas stood in silence contemplating the offer.

Saul interrupted his thoughts, "*Well, what's it going to*

TRUTH?... POSSIBLE?... PERHAPS?

be? Or are you willing to go to jail or die for him? Do you really believe what he says and does? you know that if he was from God, he would not be speaking nonsense statements like. "God is my Father" and "I came from God." How can that be? We all know his father, Joseph, and the rest of his family. Also, he has broken many of our religious rules. How can he be righteous if he does wrong?"

Judas did not know what to say, his mind went blank his hands got sweaty and responded, "*sir everything you said has taken place I cannot deny it but I don't know if I can do what you're asking me*"

Saul got up from his seat and his associates also rose. Saul said, "*Well, don't say we didn't warn you,*" he continued, "*let's go gentlemen, we have been more than fair with this man. His end is his choice.*" Judas frantically stopped them from leaving saying, "*please--- wait! Ok, I'll do it. But you must promise that you'll arrest only him...no one else. And, um... did you mention 30 pieces of silver?*"

Saul answered, "*Yes.*" "*Fine. I'll do it,*" said Judas, "*You must give me some time because it's not going to be easy. Forgive me for asking, but do you have the 30 pieces of silver, now?*"

Saul motioned with a nod to his assistant to give Judas the silver pieces. Saul said, "*You must keep us informed weekly on how things are developing. We understand it may not be an easy choice for you. Although, your eyes shining at those pieces of silver say otherwise!*"

Saul and the rest of the Pharisees left Judas' house. From that moment on, Judas sought an opportunity to betray Jesus.

Meanwhile, Jesus' fame continued to grow. Jesus was so pursued that often he couldn't walk freely due to the crowds. Jesus would get up early and isolate himself to pray.

When one of the Jewish feasts was approaching, Jesus entered a village to find crowds quickly surrounding him to hear him speak. Jesus spoke words of life to them. While speaking, Jesus noticed a young boy pressing through the multitude of people. The boy said to Jesus, "*Sir, your mother and brothers are outside this crowd. They've sent me to tell you to come home. They also said to be careful with the religious leaders.*" Jesus asked, "*Who is my mother and who are my brothers?*" Jesus answered his own question by saying, "*These are my brothers and sister who do the will of my father in heaven.*" He continued to speak to the crowds about the Kingdom that God had prepared for them. His message brought a living hope to a nation that for years had been oppressed and conquered by the Romans. When the young boy returned to Jesus' family and related the words that Jesus had spoken, his brothers were offended. James said to his mother and his other siblings, "*What are we still doing here? Let's go! This brother of ours has gone delusional he speaks as a madman!*" James made such a statement because his family and he struggled to believe what Jesus said to the people every day. However, deep in their hearts, they knew there was something special about Jesus. Their mother had told them several times the story of Jesus' birth. They witnessed the miracles he performed. No one could deny that he was very special to Israel. It was his message that they couldn't wrap their minds around. It was difficult to understand.

When Jesus' siblings arrived at home, Mary gathered her family and said, "*Listen to me, I know things are not easy for our family. I understand that we are in great danger of the Pharisees, but we must stay together and support one another! I know that some of your feelings are*

TRUTH?... POSSIBLE?... PERHAPS?

hurt by what Jesus, your brother, said when he questioned, 'who were his brothers and sisters.' But you must believe me, he does not mean to do us harm. You see how the people love him and follow him. They are not even blood relatives. How much more should we love him?"

James said, "*Mom, with all due respect, we hear what you're saying. But we cannot help fearing for our lives. Our safety is in jeopardy. You have quickly forgotten what he did about six months ago. He went into the temple and overturned the tables of the money changers and those who did business! You've forgotten that some of the merchants came to knock at our door and complain about his actions and demanded we pay for the damages Jesus caused. What about when the Pharisees came to warn us to keep him home if we knew what was good for us? You cannot forget that my dad is no longer with us and as your son, I am responsible for the well-being of our family.*"

Mary responded, "James my son, I understand, but I'm still your mother! Even tho*ugh your father Joseph is no longer with us, I promised him before his death that I would take care of our children...and I have. I also understand how you, your brothers, and your sisters feel. But God will be with us. He will protect us. He did not give me this child to cause us harm, but through him many will believe in the God of Israel.*" Mary finished speaking and everyone remained silent. They knew they had to stay together and that their mom was right. Time had passed and it was four months before the feast of palms. The people of Israel although governed by the Romans were still able to celebrate their feast. This year they seemed to have more reason because Jesus spoke about the new and upcoming Kingdom of God, they had a new hope.

Jesus was followed by some of those that followed Barabbas and even by some of the followers who at one time followed John. This new hope Israel experienced was different. John never proclaimed that he was the deliverer, he was just the one preparing the way for Jesus. John always said there was one coming behind him who he was unworthy to even undo his sandals.

As the feast of the Jews grew near, Jesus returned to his mother's house to celebrate. What a joy it was for Mary to welcome her son home and receive him safe. Jesus stayed for a few days before the feast. During dinner while sitting with his family James asked Jesus, "*Are you going to the feast?*"

Jesus answered, "*Well, I haven't thought about it.*"

James said, "*You should go and attend the feast. So that more people will see the works that you're doing. No one does anything in secret while he himself seeks to be known openly. If you do these things everyone will know who you are.*" James had said this because he and his brothers didn't believe in Jesus.

Jesus responded, "*My time has not yet come, but your time is always ready. They don't hate you, but they hate me because I testify of their evil deeds.*" When Jesus said these words James and his brothers were bothered by his comment. They decided to go ahead of him, they preferred not to be seen with him.

Mary said, "*Jesus forgive your brothers they don't know what they do.*" Jesus replied, "*don't worry mother I understand that a prophet is not welcome among his own house.*"

Jesus left the next day; he met with his disciples to arrive together into town for the feast. When they got into town they went up to the temple and Jesus saw the multitudes. The Pharisees, burning with hate, smirked at him from a distance. Jesus knew that they did not like him and wanted to kill him, but he kept speaking about the new and coming Kingdom of God.

When nightfall came, Jesus and his disciples went to the outskirts of town into Matthew's house. Matthew had worked for the government of Rome and was well off. His home was big enough to accommodate everyone for the night. Judas excused himself because he had to go home and tend to some personal matters. So, he said.

When Judas got home it wasn't long before the Pharisees knocked at his door. "*Yes, who is it?*" Judas asked. "*Open this door Judas!! Who do you think it is?!*" Saul the Pharisee answered. Judas quickly opened the door and said, "*Quickly. Come in and take a seat.*"

Saul immediately answered with authority, "*Don't tell us to hurry up! You should be the one to hurry up and give us Jesus! It has been three weeks and we haven't heard from you*"

"*I know, I know.*" Judas continued, "*It's just been hard to get away, plus all this time there has not been an opportunity. We are always among the public and I don't think it's the best time to arrest him; tomorrow after the feast, Jesus mentioned that he wanted to go to the Garden of Gethsemane that is at the outskirts of town, you know where that is... yes?... at the Garden would be the right place for you to arrest him because it would only be him and us twelve.*"

Saul looked to his group with satisfaction and fulfillment, and said, "It's dark there, not much light, how will we know who Jesus is? Remember, I promise you we wouldn't hurt anyone else, we will only arrest Jesus"

Judas assured Saul, "*I'll go ahead of you gentlemen, far enough to where you can make out what I'm doing. Whomever I kiss on the cheek is Jesus.*"

TRUTH?... POSSIBLE?... PERHAPS?

Saul warned Judas, "*This better work. If it doesn't, we will come after all of you!*" Saul and his associates got up and left.

The next day, Judas made his way to Matthew's house where Jesus and the rest of his disciples were. Judas' mind was preoccupied. Judas was reasoning within himself, justifying why he was betraying Jesus. He was convincing himself that he was doing the right thing. Heading towards Matthews's house, he walked through a small marketplace where a few of the vendors were selling fruit and bread. At the end of the vending strip he noticed an old woman selling lambs. As he got closer to the woman, he noticed she was segregating a particular lamb from the group. Judas asked, "*Having trouble ma'am?*" The lady answered, "*No, but this lamb is creating trouble among the group that I have here, and I don't want to have the rest of my lambs agitated and disrupted by this one which is causing trouble. No one will buy my livestock; they may think there is something wrong with all of them when it's just this unruly lamb.*"

Judas walked away and continued his journey, suddenly a strong devil wind enveloped him, but as quickly as it came, it quickly left. Something from that wind entered Judas, something evil. At that very moment he was totally convinced that his decision of turning in Jesus was the correct one.

When Judas arrived at Matthew's place, he received a warm welcoming. He was a friend and companion within the group. Judas had been with the team for three years; they were always together.

After their meal Jesus rose from the table and said, "*Let us go. My time has come, and the hour of the prince of this world has also come. But he has nothing on me. For*

TRUTH?... POSSIBLE?... PERHAPS?

my Father is with me. But you, will have offended me and will leave me when I most need you." Peter, his most loyal disciple, disagreed saying, *"Sir, I would never leave you! I'm ready to die for you even if these others are not!"* Jesus turned to him and replied, *"Peter, your intentions are good, but the prince of this world will shift all of you. You will deny me, and the rest will leave me."*

Judas asked, *"What about me?"* Jesus replied, *"There are some things that are better not to say, but whatever you're going to do, do it quickly."* Judas' face dropped but the other apostles didn't notice because they were so confused about what Jesus was saying.

Jesus continued, *"Let us rise and go to the feast!"* They all got up and made their way to the feast toward Jerusalem. As they got close to the entrance of town, Jesus saw a colt and a donkey tied and asked two of his disciples to untie the donkey. Jesus instructed that if anyone should question the action, they should respond,*"The master has need of them."* Jesus and his disciples entered Jerusalem. Jesus entered on the donkey as multitudes gathered around him and threw their coats on the road for the donkey to tread as if welcoming a King. They people also waved palm branches in a celebration as they welcomed the new King of Israel.

Jesus and his disciples once again went to the temple and Jesus began to teach the people about the Kingdom of God and its righteousness. In the late evening, Jesus and his disciples made their way to the Garden of Gethsemane to be away from the crowds. Once again, Judas excused himself from the others and said that he will meet up with them later because of some personal business he had to attend. Jesus said to him, "Go and do what you must my friend" those words cut Judas at heart, but his mind was already made up about his doings.

TRUTH?... POSSIBLE?... PERHAPS?

Jesus and the eleven disciples arrived at the place called Gethsemane and darkness had covered the sky Jesus said, "*All of you stay here keep watch for yourself and for me, continue praying so that we can stay vigilant before man and before God. I will go a little farther from you to pray with my Father.*" The disciples looked at each other as if to say to one another "*what is Jesus referring to?*" Jesus many times spoke to them in parables, a message of moral truth hidden in a simple story, so they did what their teacher said.

The long walk and long day exhausted the disciples and they began to fall asleep while Jesus prayed. He came back to his disciples and found them asleep. Jesus woke them and asked, "*Are you all asleep? Couldn't you keep guard for one hour?*" As he was still speaking a mob of people with torches, swords and clubs appeared. Not one of the disciples knew what was taking place since they were still slowly waking from their slumber.

Judas headed the mob and just as he had instructed the Pharisees, "*Whom I kiss that's him. Arrest him only and let us all go.*" Judas approached Jesus and kissed him in the cheek and said, "*Teacher.*" Jesus replied, "*My friend and my confidant, you've done what was written about you. I forgive you, go and let me be.*" As soon as Jesus whispered those words in Judas' ear, immediately the guards arrested him.

The Pharisees had gone to the Roman authorities and accused Jesus of many things that caused concern. Particularly, because Jesus proclaimed to be the King of the Jews. Herod was not having that. Pilot, the governor, sent a crew of soldiers with the Jewish religious leaders to arrest Jesus and the disciples, they did not know what to do half asleep and confused they all ran from the mob and dispersed each one his own way.

TRUTH?... POSSIBLE?... PERHAPS?

JESUS AND BARABBAS MEET

After Jesus' arrest he was taken to Pontius Pilot, the governor of Judea, who was very curious to meet him since he had heard so much about him. Pilot began to interrogate Jesus; he sized him up and down and asked, "*Are you the King of the Jews?*" But Jesus would not answer a word. Pilot persisted, "*Are you the King of the Jews? Do you have anything to say about yourself? Why aren't you answering me? Don't you know who I am? I have the authority to keep you or to free you!*"

Jesus finally spoke by responding to him, "*The authority you have has been given to you by my Father in heaven.*"

Pilot insisted on getting an answer out of Jesus, Pilot pressed him about the rumors and the accusations made about him being the King of the Jews. Pilot continued with the questioning. "*Are you the King of the Jews? What do you say about yourself? Your own people are saying these things about you, and you don't answer? Do you realize that it is your own people accusing you and have turned you in?*"

Jesus responded, "*My Kingdom is not from this world*".

Pilot answered, "*So you are a King?*" But Jesus stood in silence.

It became evident to Pilot that the accusations that were made against Jesus were not enough to keep Jesus arrested. He wanted to release him. Pilot called on the

TRUTH?... POSSIBLE?... PERHAPS?

Pharisees and said to them, "*This man has not done anything wrong I haven't found any reason to arrest him.*"

Saul, the spokesman of the Pharisees, said to Pilot, "*Sir, if you let him go, you're going to make Herod your enemy. For this Jesus claims that he is the King of the Jews.*"

Pilot knew that Jesus was being accused because of the Pharisees' jealousy. He decided to behave like a good politician and arranged a meeting with Herod, the King, to find out what he thought.

When Pilot and Herod met, Pilot found favor before Herod. Keep in mind that prior to this meeting, Herod and Pilot had different political views; the controversy that was created by Jesus caused them to communicate with one another.

Herod was interested in hearing about this, King of the Jews; he was curious about Jesus, but he also feared that if the rumors were true, that Jesus was indeed a King, then Herod's own Kingship would be in danger.

Herod considered the matter and everything Pilot had to say about there being no threat to his Kingdom. He understood that the only threat was upon the Pharisees and their own religious laws. Herod agreed with Pilot, he said to him, "*Pilot I found no threat to my Kingdom and I'm thankful to you for showing me your concerns. We should see each other with our wives over dinner soon.*"

Pilot answered, "*Sir, it would be an honor, I would like that.*"

Pilot, like any politician, saw the opportunity to advance his political career and was pleased that based on the situation caused by Jesus he had been able to have a good standing with Herod the King.

Pilot returned to Jerusalem and summoned the Pharisees to discuss the matter further. He said to them, "I took the matter to King Herod and he has not found the accusations threatening nor important. So, I'll tell you what I will do. I will punish him by scourging him publicly and then I will let him go"

This did not please Saul or the Pharisees. Saul responded, "*My companions and I insist that you must crucify him!*"

Pilot decided to think about this matter, as a politician he always wanted to be popular and please the people he governed. He dismissed Saul and the other Jesus accusers to reconsider the request to crucify Jesus.

Pilot called the escorting soldiers to take Jesus to the cell. Maybe it was fate or purposely the squad threw him in John's old cell---right next to Barabbas.

Barabbas heard the guards throw a new prisoner next door to him and was curious about who his new neighbor was. Barabbas called out, "Hey you, who are you and what are you in here for?"

Jesus answered, "*Who wants to know?*"

"*Barabbas is the name,.*" said Barabbas, but Jesus interrupted him before he could finish his sentence and said, "*Jesus Barabbas the leader of the insurrection. Jesus Barabbas which means, son of the Father the deliverer.*"

When Barabbas heard Jesus' words, he didn't know what to think, he didn't know how or where Jesus heard about him. Barabbas said, "That is correct. What about you... who are you?"

Jesus answered, *"I am Jesus of Nazareth."*

When Barabbas heard that name, he didn't know what to say or how to respond. He quickly composed himself and mockingly said, "Wait...don't tell me you're here for speaking the truth just like John? Your friend John occupied that cell that you're in. What's happening out there are they arresting all the preachers? Hahaha."

Jesus responded, "*Maybe God has some unfinished business with you which is why he keeps bringing us preachers right next to you.*"

Barabbas laughed changed to seriousness and said, "What would you know? Like I told John, I tell you the same, if God was involved in all of this why are His people still oppressed and governed by Rome? Where is the God of Moses, where is the God of David? Is He sleeping?

Jesus answered, "*I see you care for the people of Israel, so there is a piece of your heart that is good and wants to help others. God has unfinished business with you my friend*"

When Barabbas heard those words, his conscience was cut and his heart convicted unto righteousness, his mind began to race, and he remembered his parents' words about how special his birth had been and how special he was to God. Barabbas tried to shake those feelings off. Jesus' words kept resounding deep within him. Barabbas had been forgotten by those who at one time gave him their loyalty. Those that he called family. He had not received a visit in a long time.

Barabbas said, "*Well, maybe you're right. But what about John? Why didn't you deliver him? Why did he have to go out like that?*"

Jesus replied, "*John went out the way he chose, standing for what he believed.*"

Barabbas remembered that those were the same words he himself had said to Gestas and Dimas. Jesus

TRUTH?... POSSIBLE?... PERHAPS?

explained, "*You see Barabbas, one doesn't live until he first dies for what he believes. John is not dead he still lives in the minds and the hearts of those who knew his cause which is what he died for, and that includes you. You were that person at one time. You were willing to die for what you believed, but something happened to you. You allowed this prison to shut down your heart, but don't fear. God is not done with you yet, he sent me to preach the good news to the poor and set the captives like you free*"

Barabbas responded, "*You remind me so much of my friend John, I sure miss him. The others on this cell block and I often talk about him and how he changed even the living conditions that this prison offered us. Now they treat us with a little more decency and respect. The food is a little better and the Roman guards show us more kindness. John was always singing towards the end of his days. He would get close to his cell door and speak about righteousness and repentance by believing in the promises of God*"

Jesus answered, "*It seems to me that John was not a prisoner of his circumstances. He was a free spirit and spoke freely. You, Barabbas, are not far from being free as John*"

Again, Barabbas was convicted in his heart. that Jesus' tone of voice would speak to him as if God in heaven were calling him unto repentance of the anger that boiled inside of him, and of his unforgiveness towards those that have done him wrong.

Barabbas said, "*I'm going to see if I can sleep a little. Thank you for talking to me.*"

Barabbas went to his bunk and experienced a peace that he had not felt before. A peace that made him feel that everything was going to be alright. For the very first time in a long time he began to talk to God in his heart, and he also began to face his feelings towards Him. Barabbas said within his heart, "*I am sorry God, please forgive me.*" Immediately he felt a weight lift from him, and he fell asleep.

When Barabbas returned to his bunk, Dimas and Gestas called out to Jesus. They'd been listening to the conversation he had with Barabbas. Prison is a cold, dingy, concrete box and there is no privacy in the cell block where the prisoners live. Gestas who was the most aggressive an unreasonable said, "*Hey Jesus welcome to your Kingdom.*" He laughed mockingly as he continued to speak, "*Hey Jesus, whatever you did to get in here with us, I got to give it to you. You sure gave everyone out there a run for their money. But now, you're here with us so might us well make yourself at home.*"

Jesus answered, "*My home is not from this world. It never was. I was sent here by my Father in heaven to reconcile those that believe in him.*"

Gestas said, "*Well, good luck with that. Now that you're here, I'm sure many will believe.*" He laughed.

Jesus replied, "*Yes, many will believe. But not because I'm in here, but because I lay down my life and take it back up again.*"

Gestas said, "*What was that riddle about? At least John was clear when he spoke to us, but you sound off in the head.*"

Jesus answered, "*You don't understand because you don't believe.*"

Dimas called from his cell, "*I believe.*"

Gestas shouted, "*Shut up Dimas! Don't tell me you got converted?*" He laughed scornfully.

TRUTH?... POSSIBLE?... PERHAPS?

Dimas said," *Gestas, didn't you see God's hand in how he kept us and spared our lives? Did you forget the many times we could have been dead? It was so many times, if you think about it. Somehow some way, we didn't lose our lives in the life of crime that we carried out*"

Gestas responded, "*You're crazy. We were just that good! We had luck on our side.*"

Dimas said, "*Luck? Luck couldn't save us this time Gestas.*" Gestas became silent and went back to his bunk and lay down.

Dimas asked Jesus, "*Jesus what's going to happen to us? Are you bringing your Kingdom now? Are we going to be free from this place?*" Jesus answered, "*Yes. We are going to be free from this place not many days from now*"

Dimas did not realize that Jesus was talking about the type of death they were going to experience. Dimas said, "*I believe that, sir.*" Suddenly, the cell block door in the hallway opened. It was the Romans guards that were passing the last meal of the day.

JESUS BARABBAS CONVERSION

Next day in the morning Barabbas, called on Jesus, "*Jesus, Jesus are you awake?*"

"*Yes, I am.*" Jesus answered

Barabbas said, " *I heard you tell Dimas that you will establish the Kingdom of Israel. When will that be?*"

Jesus replied, "*Not many days from now but the truth about the Kingdom is that it's inside of us*"

Barabbas was confused by the way Jesus spoke. Barabbas wasn't used to someone speaking to him in riddles. Barabbas asked, "*What do you mean by inside of us?*"

Jesus answered, "*Unless you are born again you will not see the Kingdom of God.*"

Barabbas was frustrated. "*Would you talk to me more clearly? Why can't you talk like John? He said what he meant and, meant what he said!*"

Jesus said, "*You must die to the old you. The Barabbas that at one time ran from God and wanted to do things his own way. Instead run to God and start to do things God's way*"

Barabbas asked, "*And how can a man do that?*"

Jesus answered, "*You must admit the need for God's Spirit in your life and live for Him. Become a carrier of his Kingdom and his good news which are that man needs to repent and turn to God*"

TRUTH?... POSSIBLE?... PERHAPS?

Barabbas said, "Jesus, I hear what you're saying. *But God doesn't want me as one of his carriers of his Kingdom's good news*". Jesus asked, *"Why would you say that Barabbas?"*

Barabbas answered, "**Well, I lie. I've hurt people in the past, and besides that I'm here for a murder and I am guilty of it! I can't see God using someone like me, I'm nothing like John or you.**" As soon as Barabbas finished his sentence, the doors of the hallway to the cell block were opened. Two Roman guards entered and walked directly to Jesus' cell and escorted him out.

Barabbas shouted at the Romans guards to leave Jesus alone and to take him instead. For Barabbas remembered what happened to John. They had taken John and they never brought him back. Barabbas kept shouting at them to take him instead. Jesus turned and said to Barabbas, "**Barabbas, let it be this way. For it has to be this way so that I may fulfill my Fathers will.**"

Barabbas said, "**No! You must reign and establish Israel's Kingdom! Let them take me I'll pay the penalty you must reign. The people need you!**" Jesus turned his face from Barabbas and watched the Romans guards escort him out.

They walked down a long corridor Jesus asked, "*Where are you taking me?*", and one of them said, "*Pilot wants to talk to you, again*"

Once they got in front of Pilot, Pilot looked at Jesus up and down and said, "*Let's try this one more time. Are you the King of the Jews?*"

Jesus answered by saying, "*I am, but my Kingdom is not from this world. If it were, I could have ordered a legion of angels and my father in heaven would not have allowed you to touch me."* Pilot answered, *"Your people are the ones that turned you in. Don't you forget that. I have no business with your religious laws or customs, and from what I understand one of your own betrayed you. I spoke with the Pharisees and told them I would punish you and release you."*

Jesus did not respond.

Pilot asked, *"Are you not going to defend yourself? Aren't you going to say anything?"* Jesus refused to answer and remained quiet.

Pilot sent him back to his cell. When the door of the cell block opened and Barabbas saw Jesus being escorted back, he said, *"Hey, hey everyone, Jesus is back!!, They brought him back!!"*

Once Jesus was in his cell, he addressed Barabbas and asked, *"What was that? Were you not afraid of screaming at the Roman guards when they took me? Couldn't you see that they could have killed you?"*

Barabbas said, *"My fight with the Romans is not over I fought them before, and I will continue to fight them in every opportunity I have"*.

Jesus said, *"The Kingdom of my father does not consist of fighting the way you think. For the weapons of our warfare are not carnal but mighty through God. It is God's will that none should perish but that all might be saved"*

Barabbas asked, *"How are we saved? Can't you see where we are? This is death row if you haven't noticed. None of us are going to be saved"*

Jesus responded, *"Anyone can be saved, if they just believe."*

Barabbas silently walked back to his bunk bed and

TRUTH?... POSSIBLE?... PERHAPS?

under his breath he said, "*I believe.*" Barabbas thought no one had heard him until he heard Jesus say, "*I know you do.*" Barabbas asked, "What are you talking about?"

Jesus said, "*Come back here to your cell door.*"

Barabbas got close to his cell door and asked, "*What is it?*"

Jesus said, "*I know you believe. Barabbas you never stopped believing in the Kingdom of God you just never understood that Gods deliverance comes from heaven. By the way, did you forget that your real name is Jesus Barabbas? Just so that you don't ever forget, your name means the son of the father, the deliverer and that's who you always were and will always be.*"

Barabbas said, "*That is correct. What you're not correct about is that I can't be that deliverer anymore. You and I will die here.*"

Jesus said, "*For this reason I came to die. For you and mankind to be saved. Now you're saved Jesus Barabbas.*" After that Jesus went to his bunk bed and got on his knees to pray. Barabbas said, "*Wait what do you mean? What do you mean?*" But there was no answer from Jesus.

That day was one of the longest days for Barabbas; he couldn't stop thinking of the words Jesus spoke. Particularly, the part when Jesus reminded him of the meaning of his name, "*the son of the father, the deliverer.*"

Meanwhile, Pilot summoned for Saul and the rest of the Pharisees into his courtyard; when they arrived Pilot address them and again said, "*For the second time, I interrogated Jesus, the King of the Jews. "Saul interrupted immediately saying, "He is no King to us!*'

Pilot, raising his hand to stop Saul from talking answered,

TRUTH?... POSSIBLE?... PERHAPS?

"*Whether he is or not, I have not found anything wrong to justify him being here. I will punish him and let him go*"

A very angry Saul accused and threatened, "*If you let him go, you're not a friend of King Herod!! Jesus claims he is the King and Herod is our King. So, crucify him and let his blood be on us and on our children!*"

After much debate Pilot asked for water in a basin; he washed his hands in front of all of them and declared, "*I wash my hands of this wrong and offer an alternative for your consideration. I free a prisoner during this time of your feast; with this custom in mind, tomorrow, I will bring Jesus and another prisoner. You and all of Israel can choose who you want released.*"

TRUTH?... POSSIBLE?... PERHAPS?

BARABBAS THE DELIVERER

The next morning the doors of the hallway to the cell block opened and the Roman guards took Jesus. As he was escorted out all the prisoners in the cell block made a big commotion, they began to bang on their cell doors screaming at the top of their lungs. The Romans guards moved quickly taking Jesus out to the courtyard to face Pilot sitting on his seat of governing. Pilot faced the crowd of Jews already filling the courtyard to release the prisoner that he was accustomed to release. Pilot commanded the people to be silent said, "*everyone within the sound of my voice, you know that every year I release one of the prisoners for you and today is no exception.*" The people responded by shouting in celebration and agreement, Pilot gave a command with his hands to the guards to bring the prisoner out and set him beside him. The guards quickly pushed and shoved Jesus onto the platform before all and set him at the right hand of Pilot. The crowd shouted and made much noise, Pilot silenced the crowd and addressed the people by saying, "*I present you Jesus the King of the Jews*"

Now, Saul and the Pharisees had already manipulated the crowd to chant to crucify Jesus, so the people cried out, "*crucify him!!*" Saul shouted, *"He is not our King, Herod is our King!"* and Pilot directing his question to the people asked, "*Should I crucify your King?*" The crowd of people started chanting, "*Crucify him!! Crucify him!!*" They cried out, just as they had been ordered by Saul and the religious leaders. Pilot bid them with his hands to quiet down and he again addressed the crowd by asking, "*But what wrong has he done?*" Saul burst "*He claims to be the son of God and that's blasphemy!!!*" This started up the crowd again and they started chanting to crucify him. Pilot commanded the guards to come and he whispered to the guard who was in charge, "*Bring me Barabbas.*" The guards made their way to the death row cell block.

Inside the cell block, Barabbas heard the door open and Barabbas saw that the guards came in without Jesus. Barabbas and the other prisoners started questioning the guards about the Jesus' whereabouts, but the guards gave them no answer. They opened Barabbas' cell and escorted him out. Everything was happening so fast that Barabbas didn't know what was taking place he frantically asked, "*Hey wait, where you taking me? What's going on here? Hey, wait you can't do this!*"

The guards didn't provide him with any response. They continued to walk him from corridor to corridor. Death row was a cell block that had been built underground, it was a dungeon for those that were the worse of the worse. As they approached the door getting closer to the outside courtyard Barabbas could hear the people shouting, they were chanting, "*Crucify him, crucify him!*" It never crossed his mind that they were talking about Jesus. Barabbas quickly concluded that those chants were for him. He took a deep breath and full of courage he settled in his mind that this was the end for him. The doors to the courtyard opened and he saw the crowds of people and Jesus standing at the right hand of Pilot.

Pilot quieted the crowd as Barabbas was being pushed and shoved by the Romans guards and set him on the left hand of Pilot. Pilot said, "*Everyone now listen, I present to you Barabbas, a murderer and a thief. You decide. Should*

TRUTH?... POSSIBLE?... PERHAPS?

I release Barabbas? Or should I release Jesus in whom there is no fault?"

Saul cried out, "*Release Barabbas! We want Barabbas!!*" and the crowd followed along with Saul, "*Release Barabbas, we want Barabbas!*" Barabbas couldn't believe what was taking place right before his eyes. Barabbas looked at the crowds and at Pilot in astonishment. Then his eyes locked with Jesus. Suddenly, Barabbas understood Jesus' words. It was very clear to him why Jesus said, "*Today you are saved.*"

Barabbas continued to shake his head in disbelief. He knew what was taking place was not right. Suddenly, his mother's words resonated and reminded him of who he was meant to be. The words of John also came to mind and confirmed what he was feeling. He was feeling forgiven and alive again; the words of Jesus also echoed in his heart. In that precise moment, among the chaos of the crowd, Pilot, the guards and everything around him he was filled with peace. He felt purpose once again. It was as if he was being born again!

It was so odd that in the middle of a shouting mob, false accusations, and condemnation he would find the freedom in his soul. Suddenly, he returned to reality as he heard the words of Pilot breaking through his daze. "*Barabbas, you are free to go. Go no one will stop you. Go on and get out of here before I change my mind.*" Barabbas bolted off the platform and ran through the crowd, pushing and shoving people aside just to get through. Barabbas felt that what was taking place couldn't be real. He ran through people still chanting, "*Give us Barabbas and crucify Jesus!*" He kept shoving people away. It was so difficult to break loose through the crowds of people. People pushed him back and almost smothered him. There were so many people. Suddenly, he felt a different touch. Someone had grabbed

TRUTH?... POSSIBLE?... PERHAPS?

him saying, "*I didn't mean to do this! He is innocent, he is innocent*" Barabbas couldn't see the person's face, but the voice had regret. Barabbas looked at the face of a man he did not know, however he knew he was in turmoil. Barabbas wasn't sure what to do as the man kept repeating, "*I didn't mean to do this, he is innocent he is innocent!*" The man threw a bag of silver coins at Barabbas and ran away.

Barabbas started to run again. He felt as if everything was moving in slow motion, all he wanted to do was to get away. He did not know where, but Barabbas just needed to get away from the mob of people. He kept running until he couldn't run anymore. He was far away. He didn't know where he was, but he didn't hear the chanting of the mob anymore. He felt safe again.

The next day he traveled to Damascus. It wasn't very far from where the mob was, but it was far enough from the madness.

A few days passed and already rumors of Jesus' crucifixion had reached Barabbas. Barabbas also learned that Dimas and Gestas had been condemned and crucified next to Jesus. The rumors also suggested that Jesus' body was stolen from the grave. However, others said that Jesus had risen from the grave and that he was alive. Barabbas remembered that John, just like Jesus, had said something about being resurrected from the dead. Remembering their words brought a living hope to Barabbas.

Damascus was a city where Barabbas felt safe. He quickly settled in by finding a job as a silversmith. For once in his life Barabbas felt free from danger not having to constantly look over his shoulder. He couldn't shake one thing; the feeling that he had a significant purpose in life. While he performed his job duties, every time he would hit the iron to shape it with his hammer it was as if God was calling him for his higher purpose. His purpose and destiny were being revealed to him. Soon enough he attended the town synagogue. He became a faithful member of the congregation. He continued to grow in spirit and as the leader he was born to be. He made himself useful and allowed the Rabbis to take him under their wing; they instructed him to study the scriptures and the more he read to them his purpose became more real.

One evening as he lay reading the writing of Isaiah the prophet:

He was oppressed and He was afflicted, yet He opened not His mouth; He was led as a lamb to the slaughter, and as a sheep before its shearers is silent, So He opened not His mouth. He was taken from prison and from judgment, and who will declare His generation?"

This portion of scripture captivated him. Barabbas thought to himself, "*This is talking about Jesus, I don't know how I know that, but I just know. I know that it's talking about Jesus, but I also know is talking to me and I will declare his generation!*" Barabbas fell asleep. As he slept, in a dream, Jesus appeared to him and repeated what He told him in prison, "*You are saved.*"

When morning came it was a different kind of morning for Barabbas. He had a spring in his step! Barabbas had received and found a new revelation of his purpose to life! Barabbas began to declare the good news of God's Kingdom to his generation and the salvation of God through Jesus. Barabbas was echoing John and Jesus; he had become a Preacher just like them. As he was graced, many heard him and many in Damascus followed him. Damascus was experiencing a Kingdom revival! The news about the conversion of an entire city got to the ears of Saul.

TRUTH?... POSSIBLE?... PERHAPS?

Barabbas not only became a preacher of the Kingdom of God, but he also lived up to his name, "**Jesus Barabbas, the son of the father, the deliverer.**" The legend goes on to say that Damascus was the birth of greatness and freedom, Barabbas left a legacy and his own writing about the man called Jesus.

THE END

Which messiah do you choose? Which Kingdom do you want?

¡Como desarrollar la vida **de poder!**

LIBROS DEL
APÓSTOL
ARMANDO
Rodríguez

¡Todo lo que puedes necesitar para mejorar tu vida espiritual!

Envíanos un e-mail con tu orden ó conéctate en nuestro sitio web.

LA PROFESIA vs La Oficina Profetica

EL NOVIAZGO

BARRABAS
Armando Rodríguez

📞 (310) 834-9376   🌐 www.ensupoder.com   ✉ enpoder@yahoo.com   📍 602 Broad Ave. Wilmington CA

¡Como desarrollar la vida **de poder!**

DESENMASCARANDO EL ESPIRITU DE FAMILIARIDAD
ARMANDO RODRIGUEZ

¿EL DIVORCIO ES PECADO?
ARMANDO RODRIGUEZ

IS DIVORCE SIN?
ARMANDO RODRIGUEZ

Boronitas De Oro — ENRIQUECIENDO RELACIONES
Armando Rodríguez

BORONITAS de ORO — FORTALECIENDO A LOS MINISTROS

Boronitas de Oro — Para Parejas
Armando Rodríguez

📞 (310) 834-9376   🌐 www.ensupoder.com   ✉ enpoder@yahoo.com   📍 602 Broad Ave. Wilmington CA

¡Cada serie contiene de **2 a 5 Cd´s!**

El Apóstol **Armando Rodríguez** es un autor para el pueblo de Dios, como un conferencista que ha traído respuestas a las necesidades más difíciles a través de la palabra de Dios.

Para invitaciones contáctenos.

📞 (310) 834-9376   🌐 www.ensupoder.com   ✉ enpoder@yahoo.com   📍 602 Broad Ave. Wilmington CA

Copyright ©2020 En Su Poder,
602 Broad Ave. Wilmington Ca. 90744 USA.
Tel. 1-310-834-9376.

Todos los derechos reservados.